STRANGER

IN THE

WHITEHOUSE

546

THE
STRANGER SERIES

STRANGER

IN THE

WHITEHOUSE

to Russell

thank you for your

support

BRYAN M. POWELL

I Cor 15:58

9/21/14

TATE PUBLISHING
AND ENTERPRISES, LLC

Published by Tate Publishing & Enterprises, LLC

127 E. Trade Center Terrace | Mustang, Oklahoma 73064 USA
1.888.361.9473 | www.tatepublishing.com

Tate Publishing is committed to excellence in the publishing industry. The company reflects the philosophy established by the founders, based on Psalm 68:11,

"The Lord gave the word and great was the company of those who published it."

Book design copyright © 2012 by Tate Publishing, LLC. All rights reserved.
Cover design by Rodrigo Adolfo
Interior design by Ronnel Luspoc

Published in the United States of America

ISBN: 978-1-62147-327-5
Fiction / Political
Fiction / Suspense
12.08.23

Endorsements

While reading this story, I was blown away how real and 3D all the characters, scenes, and events are. I felt like I was on Air Force One, in the speeding car toward freedom, and could see the gunshots and explosions as they unfolded throughout. The Bible verses were extra credit helpers in understanding the story better as well.

If you never have heard of Bryan Powell before, after reading these books, you will never forget him. You can also read this book and enjoy it even if you've never read the first one.

I give this book five out of five stars because I believe readers have another great thriller/suspense writer to escape with like Joel Rosenberg, Ted Dekker, and Frank Peretti.

—Bradley Evans, writer/reviewer for
books and movies
music2movies@yahoo.com

Stranger in the White House is an exciting, multifaceted, suspenseful drama. The diabolical plot and extent of deception is captivating. It compels continuous reading to follow the pursuits of the main characters on their mission; enlisting the reader to be accomplice and a cheering participant. The author, Bryan M. Powell, weaves terror, emotion, ingenuity, stealth, bravery, heroism, and faith with determined resolve in this fast paced series of crucial and eventful exploits ... A riveting message, inspirational, and rewarding.

—William (Bill) G. Billups, Chief Warrant Officer (CWO2), United States Navy (Retired)

Dedication

To my patient and supportive wife, Patty, who has waited up for me more nights than I can count, and to my granddaughters, Reagan and Madison, who kept asking for the next book in the series.

To my many first readers, Brad, Courtney, and Eileen, who have saved my bacon on more than one occasion with their helpful critiques.

To my editor(s) at Tate Publishing and all those up and down the line who have worked tirelessly to get this book out in time.

And especially to the Lord; without Him, I could do nothing.

We are indeed co-laborers in the task of spreading the gospel through stories.

He is the author and finisher of my faith; I am His ready scribe.

Character Biographies

Chase Newton – investigative reporter with the *New York Times*' Washington, D.C. branch; the only man that Vice President Randall could trust with his life.

Megan Newton – Chase's wife and the woman in the eye of the storm.

Stan Berkowitz – Editor in Chief of the *New York Times*' Washington, D.C. branch; a tough no-nonsense editor that got too close to the truth.

President James F. Randall – President of the United States of America; a man with an unquestionable past and future.

Senator Max Wilcox – the President's choice to be the next Vice President; someone with connections.

Vice President Randall – the current Vice President; a hunted man.

Glenn Tibbits – retired CIA agent who kept a file on everyone.

Sheriff Conyers – the Sheriff of Beaumont, Colorado, who was in the right place at the right time.

Dr. Cleve Newberry – chief medical attendant to the President; a man who had an important role to play and he played it well.

Nurse Hodges – Dr. Newberry's assistant wasn't who she said she was.

Nguyen (Wynn) Xhu – first generation immigrant from Vietnam; was chosen to be the temporary Chief of Staff; a determined woman with one mission to fulfill.

The Dean – a man with a long shadow and a sordid past.

Prologue

Air Force One…

Vice President Randall stood before Judge Patricia Fisher of the Sixth Circuit Court of Appeals and raised his right hand and with an even voice recited the thirty-nine words that make a common citizen the next president of the United States of America; "I do solemnly swear (or affirm) that I will faithfully execute the office of President of the United States and will to the best of my ability preserve, protect, and defend the Constitution of the United States so help me God."

He smiled, shook hands with the judge, and turned to the small group of cameramen and reporters gathered in the airborne Oval Office.

President Randall took his place behind a small podium and spoke with a steady voice, without the benefit of a teleprompter.

"Today we have once again seen tragedy strike at the heart of our nation. And though sadly, it may have hit its head, it missed its heart, for you, my fellow Americans, are the heart of this great land. You are the life-force that keeps this country alive and well and free. It is this kind of determination and resolve which you demonstrate every day when you get up and go to the factories and fields of this great country that those who would seek to do us harm can never destroy. It is this kind of energy, this kind of drive, this yearning to be free which will guide us through these dark days.

"So it is with sadness and with joy I stand before you today to lead you out of the malaise of the past into a brighter tomorrow. Together we will close the chapter on the past and move forward to a future filled with hope and promise, a future filled with freedom and justice for all, and a future where our children's children will live in peace with all mankind." He looked directly into the lens of the camera with his steel-gray eyes as if he were looking into the very soul of the nation. "And we will not rest until we see that day dawn on the horizon of an earth that has been reborn. I ask you join me on this journey." With that, the forty-seventh president concluded his brief remarks.

He turned and closed his eyes and prayed to the voice inside his head.

And the voice answered, "A new day is about to dawn, but it isn't the one these poor fools dream of," he muttered to himself and smiled.

Chapter 1

The New York Times Bureau,
Washington, D.C., Monday

It was a cold and rainy April afternoon in Washington, DC, and it seemed that all of nature had joined the country in mourning. Chase Newton, an investigative correspondent with the *New York Times*, sat staring out his corner office window as the rain beat against the glass. The thoughts of the day's tragic events passed like a B-rated movie before his eyes.

His sudden rise to fame came as the result of his investigation of the Order over four years earlier. As a cub reporter with the *Beaumont Observer*, he had gone underground and discovered that the Order was a clandestine organization whose stated goal was the destruction of America. A slight chill swept over him as he reflected on those wild and dangerous days; days in which his life and the life of those he loved hung in the balance. He shuddered at the thought of how close he came to death as he raced toward the podium that fateful day with only a cigarette lighter and the document ceding half of the country to the authority of the Order. Were it not for his quick thinking, the country he knew would not be the same. He not only saved America from a disastrous chapter, but his heroic efforts also resulted in his life taking a major turn for the better.

His office, located on the eleventh floor of the Willard Building on G Street, was not far from the White House. Awards lined the walls of his palatial office. There were pictures of him and the president shaking hands, a picture of him and the governor of Colorado, and a plaque displaying his Pulitzer Prize for Investigative Journalism. There were many other awards and certificates lining his walls, but the one photograph that he was most proud of was of him and Megan on their wedding day. After all of the interviews, the sworn testimonies before House and Senate sub-committees, and hearings before the House Rules on Ethics, life as an investigative reporter returned to normal; that is, as normal as it could be commuting between New York, Washington, DC, and Beaumont, Colorado. It was during the intense undercover operation in which he had placed himself in harm's way to uncover the plot of the Order that he realized he was madly in love with Megan Richards. Megan, or M, as Chase affectionately called her, is the daughter of T.J. Richards, the pastor of the now defunct Community First Church of Beaumont and leader of the Order. His disappearance was a mystery yet to be solved; only then could he really celebrate. Suddenly, his telephone rang, jolting him back to reality. It was a back line, one that circumvented the secretary pool. Chase answered the call and sat in stunned silence while listening to the voice on the other end.

"Chase, listen to me. The man who was just sworn into the office of the Presidency is an impostor." The one speaking to Chase was one he knew well—vice president.

An hour earlier, a violent attack had taken place against the government. Insurgents plotted and carried out a plan to kill the president and succeeded.

Richard C. Donovan, the forty-sixth president, had only been in office one term and had successfully won re-election. His term in office was getting under way when he was tragically cut down. As designated by the Constitution, the line of succession called for the immediate confirmation of the vice president to the office of the presidency. How could he be an impostor? Chase asked himself. He knew Vice President Richard Donovan well. He had interviewed him on several occasions, and they had become good friends. How could someone other than the vice president be sworn into the office of the presidency without the Secret Service, the FBI, and the press knowing about it? And who is this on the phone telling this outrageous story? Chase thought.

This was all a dream—or nightmare.

Knowing only a very few people knew the daily password, Chase thought it would be a good idea to test his caller's identity. "What is today's password?" Chase asked the caller, with a slight hesitation in his voice.

"Today's password is cakewalk."

Chase breathed a sigh of relief. "It's good to hear from you Mr. Vice President," he said. "I had to be sure."

"That's okay, son. Now listen, Chase, there was not only a successful attack against the president, but there was also an attempt on my life. Obviously they failed, or I wouldn't be speaking to you. But they think I'm dead, and someone who looks just like me has just been sworn in as president of the United States. When they discover that I'm still alive, my life won't last five minutes. I've got to go into hiding, and you have got to expose this plot to take over our government," the vice president said vehemently.

Sweat beaded on Chase's upper lip as he absorbed the import of what the vice president had just said. "It's the Order again, isn't it?"

The vice president let a moment go by. "I don't know about that, son. I just know that whoever did it knew the president's and my itinerary and knew the best time to hit us," he said through an emotionally charged voice.

Chase stiffened in his seat. His mind was swirling. "Did anyone see it? Were there any witnesses?" Chase ran his fingers through his hair.

The pause seemed to stretch into an hour as Chase waited for the vice president to regain control of himself.

"Yes there were, but sadly they were eliminated, too. None of my security detail survived the attack," the vice president said. His voice thickened.

A sense of dread greeted Chase like an unwelcome guest as he listened to the vice president. He hated being embroiled in another life threatening situation, especially now that he was married. What would he tell Megan if he did? What would he say if he didn't?

"How is it that you survived, then, Mr. Vice President?" inquired Chase as he took out a notepad and started scribbling franticly. His pencil point broke and he tossed it aside.

The vice president leaned in closer to the phone. "I'll get to that in a moment, but suffice it to say, it won't be long before they learn that I am still alive," he answered succinctly.

"Well, what can I do, Mr. Vice President?" asked Chase. He could feel his pulse quicken., his breathing shorten.

"Once I am secure, I will call you and help you by giving you as much information as I can, but for now I have to go."

With that, the telephone conversation ended, and the phone went dead.

Chapter 2

The New York Times Bureau, Washington, D.C.

Where do you begin an investigation of a sitting president? Chase asked himself. *Should I walk into the Oval Office and say, "Mr. President, you are an impostor"? No, that would only get me arrested and put behind bars for a very long time. I need to get some help, but who? Who could I trust with the biggest story in the country and not blow it before I could corroborate it?*

Stan Berkowitz.

Not only did Chase benefit greatly from uncovering a plot to take over the country, but so did Stan. As editor of the *Beaumont Observer*, Stan was credited with having the savvy to know a big story when he saw one. As the result of his involvement in the undercover investigation, Stan was immediately promoted by the *New York Times* to Editor in Chief of the Washington, DC, bureau. His was an unenviable position, and there was a lot of pressure on him; thus, he put pressure on his reporters to get the facts right. As was true of him in Beaumont, so it was true of him now; he had a way of driving his reporters to new heights, or new depths, depending on your perspective.

Despite his new position, his personality hadn't changed, either; he was still just as crusty as ever.

There was one other thing that had not changed about Stan. If he thought that you were on to a big story, all the resources of the paper were behind you. Chase needed Stan, and he needed those resources now.

Chase, dressed in a golf shirt and slacks, stepped out of the elevator on the fourteenth floor. He proceeded down the wide corridor to the newspaper bureau headquarters and entered the spacious office. He was greeted by Stan's personal secretary, the ever vigilant Mrs. Hudson.

"Hello, Mr. Newton. Are you here to see Mr. Berkowitz?" Chase had not gotten used to all this formality, but he humored her by answering her question politely.

Chase nodded his head. "Yes, ma'am!"

She looked over her glasses. "Do you have an appointment?" she inquired.

"No, ma'am, but—" his sentence was cut off as she interrupted Chase mid-sentence.

"Mr. Berkowitz is a very busy man, and you can't just barge in on him like you did in the old days, Mr. Newton. You're in the big league now, and you have got to learn to go through the proper channels," Mrs. Hudson said in a condescending tone.

Chase's face reddened slightly at being spoken to as if he were a schoolboy reporting to the principal's office for detention.

You must be enjoying the power of your position, Mrs. Hudson, Chase thought. "If he's got just a few minutes,

I really need to see Stan—I mean Mr. Berkowitz—now. It's urgent," Chase said as he glanced at his Rolex watch.

Mrs. Hudson eyed him suspiciously, "Yes, well it seems that it is always urgent with you, Mr. Newton, but I'll check Mr. Berkowitz's schedule to see if I can work you in." Then she glanced down at his itinerary.

Chase was getting rather hot under the collar of his golf shirt. "Look Ms., uh, Mrs. Hudson, if you don't let me in to see Stan in one minute, I'm going to—"

The door separating Mrs. Hudson's office from Stan's swung open, and Stan stepped out. He had a gentleman in tow that Chase had never seen before. The two men shook hands and parted company with a few, "I'll be in touch," and, "Let's do lunch," type of comments. Stan nodded to Chase, and they both stepped back into Stan's office.

Chase smiled at Mrs. Hudson as she glanced up from the appointment book. A look of consternation filled her stoic face.

Stan's office made Chase's look like a kid's playroom. His was the hub of all that went on in Washington, DC, and if anyone was in the know, it was Stan.

"You look like you have seen a ghost. What's on your mind?" Stan asked as he took his seat behind his cluttered desk.

Chase hesitated, wondering if he should go out on this limb. "We've got a problem."

His face tightened. "What do you mean we? You're the investigative reporter with the Pulitzer Prize hanging on your wall."

Chase sighed. "Look, can we talk freely? I mean your office isn't bugged or anything, is it?" he said as he looked around the room.

Stan's jaw tightened. "Are you getting paranoid? You're not having flashbacks of Beaumont, are you?" he said as he crossed his arms and looked at his new Doxa watch.

With an extra effort of willpower, Chase pushed himself forward. "No, I'm not paranoid, but I am worried that if what I'm about to tell you falls into the wrong hands, we both are going to be swimming at the bottom of the Potomac River."

Stan shook his head in disbelief. "That's a pretty heavy piece of information. I sure hope you have the facts to back it up before you go and get me involved," he said as he eyed Chase wearily.

Chase put his hands on his boss's desk and leaned in closer. "You know, I've got a nose for the news, but I didn't dig this up. It came to me in the form of a phone call. You see, I just got off the phone with the vice president." Chase paused to let that sink in.

Stan blinked, as he tried to absorb Chase's last statement. "How could you do that? The president hasn't appointed one yet." His voice rose an octave. Chase shook his head. "You don't understand, and I don't think I do, either, but the man I just spoke to claimed to be Vice President Randall."

"You mean President Randall, don't you?" his boss retorted.

"Nope, Vice President Randall!" Chase said emphatically.

Stan folded his arms across his sizable chest and leaned back. "How can that be? I just watched a circuit court of appeals judge swear Vice President Randall into the office of President on Air Force One."

"It can't be. The man I spoke to was Vice President Randall, and I can prove it," continued Chase.

"And how can you prove that?" He said as his eyebrows crested in a question.

Chase shifted his gaze around the room as if to see if anyone was looking and lowered his voice.

"He gave me today's password. Only a limited number of people have access to that kind of information, and he knew it," he said with a conspiratorial tone in his voice.

Stan took out a handkerchief and wiped his forehead. "Okay, tell me what today's password is, and I'll verify it. If you are right, we have a problem!"

He grabbed a notepad. "Let me write down, but don't read it out loud." Chase said as he wrote out the word cakewalk.

Stan turned to his computer and typed in a code and waited. A screen came up, and he entered another code. He repeated this two more times before he was in the very belly of the beast. It was one of the most secure sites on the planet, and it takes a level five clearance to get into this site; Stan had it.

"Okay, let's see that password."

He picked up the piece of paper and looked at it over his newly acquired bifocals.

Stan typed in the word and waited. The monitor screen scrolled for a moment and began flashing one word in a field of black. Chase stood and stared at the monitor screen. There it was. Cakewalk.

Stan stood and tapped his chin. "Man, have we got a problem! Do you know who just left my office as you barged in?"

"No, should I?" asked Chase with a crooked smile.

Stan let a moment of silence pass. "It was Senator Max Wilcox, the president's pick for vice president. He was here to give me an exclusive before the news broke in this afternoon's press conference."

"Stan, I got a bad feeling about this. It's like déjà vu all over again."

Stan paused and chose his words carefully. "Why can't the real vice president just come forward and call a press conference himself and tell the whole world who he is and be done with it?" Stan asked.

"Because," Chase said as he waved his hands animatedly, "just after the successful attack on President Donovan, there was an attack on Vice President Randall. They—whoever they are—thought they succeeded in killing the vice president. They think the real James F. Randall is dead, and they have pulled a bait and switch on America."

"Where is James Randall now?" said Stan with tension in his voice.

"The last thing he said was that he was going into hiding and when he was in a secure place he would call me and give me all the information I would need to uncover this plot."

"Uh oh, here we go again," Stan said as he skimmed through his Rolodex for a phone number.

Forgetting the seriousness of the moment, Chase cocked his head and leaned over his boss's shoulder.

"Who are you going to call? Not Ghost Busters, I hope," he said.

Stan eyed Chase carefully as he picked up the phone. "Do you remember Glenn and his daughter, what's her name, uh, Susan, no uh, Jennifer?"

Chase's eyes widened. "Yes, how could I forget? I spent hours with that woman, pouring over meaningless numbers, and I did it without a word of complaint," said Chase with a distant glint in his eye.

"Well those numbers weren't meaningless after all."

"I'd do it again in a heartbeat if I had to," Chase interjected.

Stan just shook his head. "Well, simmer down, boy. You are a married man now," Stan said as if he had to remind Chase.

"Yes, and happily married, at that, but I was saying…"

"I know what you were saying, but just don't stir up old feelings and mess up a good thing," his boss said.

Chase lowered his eyes. "You are absolutely right, my friend, but how can Glenn and Jennifer help us now? Didn't Glenn retire from the FBI's SIU unit?" he asked as he watched Stan dial the number.

Stan nodded. "Yes, he did, but in this case we need someone who we can trust and who has the expertise to unravel this mess you got us into."

"Me!" Chase said incredulously, "How'd I do that?"

"You answered the phone, didn't you?" Stan asked as he waited for it to be answered.

Chapter 3

The White House Press Room,
Monday afternoon

The three p.m. press conference, located in the Blue Room, was a buzz with excitement as Chase took his seat and prepared for the president's big announcement; unexpectedly his cell phone vibrated. Before he could answer it, the press secretary, a holdover from the previous administration, announced the president's arrival. "All rise. Ladies and gentlemen of the press corps, may I introduce to you the president of the United States, Mr. James F. Randall."

Everyone rose as President Randall stepped into the room and strode to the podium. "Thank you, ladies and gentlemen of the press corps. You may be seated."

He paused a minute for the men and women in front of him to get settled. "It is my desire to act swiftly and decisively in naming my choice for the next vice president, after which I will take a few questions." Again he spoke without a teleprompter.

"Today I will be submitting the name," he paused to let the cameras flash and the curiosity build, "Max Wilcox as my choice for vice president. As you know, Senator

Max Wilcox has been my friend and ally for many years. You will remember when I was a senator, we crafted many key pieces of legislation together. Some of those never made it into law. Some of them died in committee or were vetoed during the Campbell administration. With my friend Senator Max Wilcox, soon to be Vice President Max Wilcox, at my side, we will bring these pieces of legislation back to the Senate and House, and I will sign them."

Both he and the senator were most liberal of their party, who look at the Constitution as an impediment to their agenda. In getting their liberal agenda implemented, America would not look the same in four to eight years.

He waited for those taking notes to catch up. He was enjoying the moment. "Now I will take a few questions from the press," he said as he scanned the group, looking for a particular hand.

The first question was a soft ball from an AP correspondent. "Mr. President, do you think Senator Max Wilcox will have any trouble being approved by the congress?"

President Randall knew the importance of appearing decisive and spoke succinctly.

"Mr. Wilcox is a well-respected member of the Senate and has been for the last twenty years. With the current majority party being moderates I see no problem with his quick approval. As a matter of fact, let me encourage the congress to act expeditiously."

He certainly looks like the man I know as James F. Randall, Chase thought as he watched the president lead the press conference.

There was a clamor of reporters, each raising their hands, hoping to be recognized like a room full of first graders.

"Yes, the woman from the Washington Post, Ms. Sanchez."

Ms. Sanchez, a seasoned correspondent, had a reputation as a hard-hitting journalist. She stood and paused long enough for all eyes to be fixated on her. Then she read her question. "Mr. President, rumor has it that before you were sworn into office, you also came under attack. Is this true?"

The president smiled and nodded before answering. "Yes, Ms. Sanchez, that rumor is quite true. However, my security detail was expecting it and was able to fend off the attackers. The limousine I was in was the second one, and the attackers thought I was in the first one. My driver broke away, and I was never in any real danger," the president said using a controlled hand motion.

"May I ask a follow-up question?" Ms. Sanchez insisted.

"Yes, go ahead, Ms. Sanchez. What is your question?" the president replied.

"Does your administration have any idea who carried out this vicious attack against both you and President Donovan?"

The president looked directly into the lens. "Let me say this." He paused and chose his words carefully. "We have our suspicions, and we are working hard on following up on them. I feel confident that we will soon learn who is behind these unprovoked and unprecedented attacks against a peace-loving country, and they will be brought to justice whether they are foreign or domestic."

The cacophony resumed as hands and voices were raised to attract the president's attention. But rather than take another question, he politely thanked the press corps, turned and walked back up the red carpet, which led to the Oval Office. The press secretary rose as the president turned to leave and stepped up to the podium.

"Thank you, ladies and gentlemen of the press. We have issued a written statement if you would kindly pick up one as you leave. We would appreciate it. You are dismissed."

By three thirty in the afternoon, the sky had cleared, and Chase returned to his office with more questions than answers. Why was the press so soft on the president? Why not ask some real questions? Who is Senator Max Wilcox really? Yes, Chase knew a little about him. Who didn't? He was a leading senator, but why choose him? Why was Max Wilcox chosen and not the majority leader? The record showed that he and Wilcox they were not the best of friends and, at times, were even political enemies. So why him? Was it political payback? Did Senator Max Wilcox know something about the new president, and this was to buy his silence? Chase wrote these questions and others in his notebook for future reference.

Again his cell vibrated with a message from Stan. "We have a nine-one-one problem."

This was Glenn and Chase's old way of communicating to each other. They had used codes such as 511 for, "Let's do lunch," and 711 for, "Get your tail in here quick." The number 911 was just as you would expect—an emergency.

Chapter 4

The New York Times Bureau,
Fourteenth Floor, Stan's Office

"Glenn?" asked Stan as he held the cell phone tight against his ear. "This is Stan Berko—"

"I know who it is," Glenn interrupted him in midstride. "What took you so long to call?" Glenn could hear the smile in his friend's voice.

Stan, rather taken aback, looked at the phone in his hand and continued, "How did you know it was me and that I would be calling?"

"It's my business to know," he said without losing a beat. "Does Chase know you are calling me?"

Stan cast a jaundiced eye toward Chase. "Yes, why?"

Glenn tilted his head back and inhaled slowly as he considered his words carefully. "Well, if this call is about what I think it is and Chase is in on it, then you guys are in deep doo-doo, and you want me to come to the rescue. Let's talk," Glenn offered.

Stan held up his fat hand as if to slow down his friend's eagerness. "No, my friend, let's not talk over the phone. By the way, do you still fish?" he inquired. Stan already knew the answer as Glenn's reputation for being an avid fisherman was well known throughout county surrounding Beaumont. Yet he asked anyway, as part of the ruse he was weaving.

"Well, yes, of course, why?" Glenn asked with growing interest.

"Well how about I send you a client friend of mine, and you take him to your best fishing hole? Let's say you two meet for breakfast tomorrow at your favorite restaurant, and you guys have a nice chat. Then you two go out and catch us some big ones," Stan said in a conspiratorial tone.

Glenn knew exactly what Stan was getting at and agreed to meet him the next day.

He and Glenn had become good friends since the ordeal involving the Order. It was Glenn and Chase, along with Glenn's daughter Jennifer (aka Susan), who broke the plot to take over half of the United States. He owed his life to Glenn, not to mention his new and very powerful position with the *New York Times*.

"Oh, say Glenn, does that lovely daughter of yours fish, too?" asked Stan casually.

Glenn thought a minute. "Yes, yes of course, as a matter of fact, she is on a fishing trip as we speak. Don't know when she'll return," he said vaguely.

"Well, give her our regards when you see her." Stan said casually.

"Okay, I'll do that. Take care, and I'll talk to you soon."

With that, they both hung up, and Chase looked at Stan.

"Why the cloak and dagger? I thought you said your office was not bugged," Chase asked with a raised eyebrows.

"It's not," Stan said looking over at a lampshade and pointing. "I was just making arrangements for a dear friend of mine to go fishing with a real pro. By the way, are you hungry?"

The sudden change of topics caught Chase somewhat off guard, but he went along. "Well, yeah, if you are buying! You want to go now? I mean, don't you have to ask Mrs. Hudson's permission or something?" Chase asked with a grin.

"Mrs. Hudson is just doing her job. She means no harm," Stan said as he wrote a quick note and gathered up some papers. He led Chase out of his office. As he stepped around his desk, Stan took a toothpick out of the corner of his mouth and placed it precariously on the edge. The slightest movement would send it to the floor. Stan gently closed his door and locked it.

"Mrs. Hudson, I'll be out of the office for about an hour or so, but you can reach me on my cell or text me. You know the codes," he said as he placed the note on her desk.

As he walked by the secretary's desk, Chase tried to think of some pithy statement to make. He decided against it; instead, he just gave Mrs. Hudson a polite smile.

Both Stan and Chase stepped out into the hall and walked to the elevator. Stan punched the button marked Parking Level and waited until the elevator doors opened. They stepped into the dark-wood-paneled elevator and waited for the doors to close. The ride to the parking deck was quiet; neither man spoke until they got to Stan's car.

Finally Chase broke the silence. "So what's happened since I was in your office last?" He asked as Stan started his car.

He hesitated a moment and shifted his weight to one side before answering. His eyes narrowed as he described the events of the morning. "This morning before you came into my office, someone bugged my office." Stan confessed as he stared ahead.

"When? How? Why?" Chase's heart skipped a beat.

Stan's expression darkened, "Well, for starters, it must have been last night," said as he pulled out on to G Street and headed east away from the White House. He turned right on 13th Street and pulled in at his favorite restaurant—the M&S Grill.

"Man, I love this place," Stan said. "Just smell those steaks and onions."

Chase wasn't hungry; at least, he wasn't until they pulled into the parking lot just two blocks from the White House.

The waitress quickly seated them in the back in a booth made from rich mahogany with a beveled glass top. After ordering Stan's favorite, an Arnold Palmer, for both of them, Chase resumed his inquiry.

"I thought you always left a toothpick or something on your desk in a certain position. If it was in a different position when you returned, that would indicate that someone had been in your office."

The etched lines in his face told more than his words. "Yes, I always leave something in my office—a toothpick, a dime, a pencil, something lying in a certain way—if it is moved, then I know someone has been in my office. But nothing was moved. That's what's got me baffled. I have standing orders. No one is allowed to enter my office if I am not present. I learned that from Ms. C," Stan said as he reflectively.

Four year earlier, Ms. Conley had left Jimmy Stevens in her office with a very important document. It cost Ms. C her life, and it was the undoing of the Order. Stan would never forget that lesson.

"So how did you discover that your office was bugged?"

Stan's gaze shifted as he spoke. "I don't know why, but I had a funny feeling that I was being watched, and so I ran a radio frequency scanner around the place. I got a reading just as I passed the lampshade on the end table."

A look of concern clouded Chase's face. "Well, why was your office bugged in the first place? You're not a criminal or some drug king pin, are you, Stan?"

Stan leaned in closer and lowered his voice. "No, but if anybody knows anything in this town, it's me. My office is the hub of what's happening in Washington."

Chase shrugged his shoulders uncomfortably. "So how much do you think whoever has been listening knows?" he probed.

Stan held his breath and let it out slowly. "They probably know what you and I know...that the real vice president is alive and in hiding somewhere and that you and I are on to them. That puts you and me in grave danger. If they are willing to kill the two most important men in the world, then they sure as heck won't stop with them. They will come looking for us as well. Now, what they plan on doing with that knowledge is a mystery to me. I just hope that they don't figure out what I was talking about when I spoke to Glenn. If they do and they have evil plans, his life may be in jeopardy, as well."

Chase ran his hand through his straw-colored hair, he felt like such an amateur. "Well why did you let me go blabbering on? You should have signaled me or something," Chase said as the waitress brought his meal.

"You blurted it out before I could stop you. That's why. I just hope they don't figure out the vice president's code name and password."

Chase cocked his head and eyed Stan speculatively.

"Okay, so who is this client you are sending to meet Glenn?" asked Chase between bites.

His boss stared back at him without blinking. "You… you are the client, and I want you on a plane by seven o'clock tonight."

Chase nearly choked on his tea. "What about Megan?" he sputtered. "I can't just fly off to Colorado without so much as a good-bye. Shouldn't I call her and let her know I won't be home for dinner?"

"Nope!" said Stan with a raised hand. "I've already taken care of it. The note I left with Mrs. H. instructed her to make the arrangements with the airline and your wife. I have asked for Megan's permission to abduct you for the next few days."

Chase leaned back with an impish look in his eyes. "Oh, really? She's that easily bamboozled, hmmm?" Chase said with a twisted smile.

"Yep!" Stan was lying, he wasn't completely honest with Megan, but he intended to clear things up just as soon as Chase was on that plane.

The flight to Denver departed at 8:10 p.m. and arrived at 11:44 p.m. without event. He arrived at Denver's busy airport, and after renting an SUV, he headed to the town of Beaumont. Chase pulled into the one hotel that still had its light on around 1:30 in the morning. He was spent from a long day and longed for his own bed. Once he got checked in, he found his room, went in, and crashed without undressing.

Chapter 5

Beaumont, Colorado

Tuesday morning came early…too early, but Chase had a busy day ahead of him. He got up, changed into a new pair of jeans, donned a flannel shirt, and laced up a new pair of hiking boots he bought in the Denver airport, and headed out to breakfast.

The Colorado air was crisp and clear as he walked the short distance from his hotel to Maxine's Diner. Chase missed eating at the old place, having spent a lot of time there during his years as a cub reporter with the *Beaumont Observer*. Back then, this was as close to home cooking as he could get, having eaten there two, sometimes three, times a day. His mind went back to the first time he met Glenn Tibbits. Never in a million years would he have imagined the changes that that one meeting would bring. Now he was going there to meet Glenn again.

He wondered what changes this meeting would bring.

It was the peak of the breakfast hour, and Maxine's Diner was packed with policemen, firemen, and utility workers. People from all walks of life made this a regular stop in the daily routine of Beaumont.

In the back sat an elderly man dressed in overalls. His snow-white hair curled out from under the fishing cap he was wearing. Several other old timers were standing around his table, laughing about something trivial. As Chase approached, the group dispersed, revealing a distinguished figure. It was Glenn, and his face was strong and lined with years of service to his country. Although the years had taken much since the last time he had seen him, to Chase, the older gentleman's eyes were still a crisp, cool blue that seemed to pierce through Chase's soul.

"Chase, it's so good to see you again. Please sit down," Glenn said with a smile as the two shook hands warmly.

Chase eyed the old diner with affection.

"Doesn't this remind you of another meeting we once had?"

"Yes, sir, it does. I was just thinking back to the first time we met here as I walked over." He paused in reflection. "I wonder what this meeting will bring," he said with a look of concern on his face.

Glenn's keen eyes gave nothing away.

"Well, the changes have already begun, and it may be up to us to change things back again."

They ordered breakfast and chatted about their lives.

"I wonder why Stan called you into this mess. Aren't you retired?" Chase asked as he mixed his scrambled eggs with his cheese grits.

The older man's eyes saddened. Too many years of snooping, of digging, of looking over his shoulder made him cynical.

"Well, there are not a lot of people up there in Washington, DC, whom I could trust. If what I think is going on is true, then I would gladly come out of retirement."

"Do you know what Stan was talking about when he called?" Chase asked between bites.

"I have been monitoring the chatter, and I have my instincts. After all, I have been in the uh…information business for a long time," said Glenn quietly.

The rest of the breakfast was eaten with a minimal of small talk as each man savored the meal and each other's company. When they had finished their breakfast, Glenn led Chase to his pick-up truck that was loaded with fishing gear. They climbed in and headed off to Glenn's favorite fishing hole.

"How's Jennifer these days?" Chase asked nonchalantly. Though he was happily married, he still remembered those long days they spent researching the backgrounds of the membership of the Community First Church.

A look of amusement filled Glenn's eyes. "Oh, she's fine. The agency has her out on assignment currently. I'm not at liberty to disclose her whereabouts at this time. You understand, don't you?"

"I thought she had a cushy desk job," Chase interjected.

Glenn shrugged in resignation. "Yeah well, the guys at the top thought they needed the best in the business. That got her out of the office and into the field after about two weeks. And they were right in doing so, if I do say so myself."

Glenn changed the subject as quickly as possible by asking about Megan. Chase filled him in on their life together as they travelled along the country road that led to Glenn's favorite fishing hole.

"Now that we've gotten caught up on the last four years, we need to talk about today's events and what we need to do to straighten things out," Glenn said as he watched the landscape change.

"Once we get out to the river, then we can talk openly," suggested Chase.

Glenn nodded his head in agreement.

Precisely twenty minutes later, they turned off the main road and bounced along a rutted, well-worn dirt road that led to the river.

Chase couldn't help but notice the shafts of sunrays as they jabbed through the protective leaf canopy like javelins and ricocheted off the shimmering stream. It was a splendid day for fishing or anything else for that matter. As much as he enjoyed the company of his old friend, he'd rather be spending it here with Megan.

Glenn pulled the truck into a thicket, which nearly obscured its presence, and got out. The two men collected their fishing gear and took a narrow path that led down to the river.

After spending the last four years in the big city, Chase was struck with the serenity of the forest. The sounds of the birds in the trees, and the babble of the water over rocks was a welcomed relief from the hustle and bustle of Washington DC life. He leaned over and scooped up some water and let it drizzle down his throat. It was cool and refreshing. He drank in the sights, the sounds, and inhaled the fresh air of the river before settling on the unpleasant task ahead of him.

Chase found a large rock to sit on while Glenn stood. And so began the real reason for Chase's visit.

"So tell me about the phone call you got from the vice president. By the way, have you heard from him since your phone call?"

Chase stared at Glenn in disbelief. "Now, how did you know about my phone call from the vice president? Did Stan tell you about it?"

Glenn's face gave away no secrets as his eyes studied Chase.

"You clearly don't know how well connected I am, do you, Chase?" he said after what seemed an eternity.

Again, Chase had the deep feeling of inadequacy as he sat before the seasoned veteran. It was clear from Chase's body language that he was uncomfortable under Glenn's benign gaze. Finally he forced an answer to the surface.

"Nope, I haven't heard a word from him since his initial call yesterday. They had just sworn in the vice president, or at least a man posing as the vice president, as president, and I got this call from a man claiming to be the real vice president. He said his caravan was ambushed and all were killed in an explosion from an IED. They thought they killed him too, but as chance would have it, he was never even in the vice president's limousine. A few minutes before the caravan left his residence, he decided to drive himself. The only other person who knows that he is alive is his personal bodyguard who was driving his car at the time of the attack. They are in hiding in an undisclosed location."

Glenn held his composure well as he digested this new information. This was a development he had not expected, and it would require a new set of ground rules to play by.

"How do you know that it was the vice president?" he probed as he cast out his first lure into the placid waters. The gentle ring of energy began where the lure landed and smoothly worked its way to where he stood.

"For starters, I asked him for the daily password. He knew it. It was 'cakewalk.'"

"So the vice president is alive, and the man who was sworn in as president is a fraud, and we have been given the job of uncovering who he is and what he is up to," Glenn said as the weight of his assignment bore down upon him. He suddenly looked tired and weary beyond his years.

"Yes, and at the same time maybe even save our nation from disaster…again."

After a moment of introspection, Glenn began to describe his activities leading up to their meeting. "I have been doing my own research on the people leading our government ever since the last fiasco. I just don't trust those people in Washington, DC. You never know who they really are and what their agenda is."

Chase gave a quick jerk of the pole he was holding, but the fish was quicker. He reeled in his line and recast it before continuing his line of thinking.

"Yeah, not after what happened with the Order. There were people in high places of government ready to sell out our country for the sake of political gain," Chase said grimly.

Glenn sighed.

"Fortunately, there were enough congressmen left to stand up for America and defend the Constitution."

"Well, how do we get enough support for impeaching a sitting president when his party is in the majority and we have such flimsy evidence?" Chase stared at Glenn questioningly.

Glenn lifted his rod and checked the live bait on his second pole. It was gone. "It will be extremely difficult, especially when it's the president of the United States who is leading the conspiracy."

Chase shook his head and wondered out loud, "Where do we begin with such a monumental task?"

Glenn thought a moment. "Well we need to discover who he really is."

"He certainly looks and talks like the real deal. How can we prove he isn't?" Chase asked with growing interest.

Glenn's eyes took on a distant look as if he were in chemistry class speaking to a group of sophomores. "DNA—or Deoxyribonucleic acid. No two people have the same DNA. Forensic scientists can use DNA in blood, skin, saliva, and hair to identify a matching DNA of any individual. The DNA profiling compares short sections of repetitive DNA between two people. It is an extremely reliable technique for identifying an individual's identity."

This was all quite rudimental to Chase and he felt a tinge of chagrin as he friend spoke. He knew Glenn meant nothing by it so he swallowed his pride and listened.

"So how do we get a sample of President Randall's DNA and compare it with the real James F. Randall's DNA?" Chase asked.

"As I said, I have been doing some extensive investigating on my own. I have files that you need to see on my—"

Suddenly a shot rang out, and Glenn fell forward, blood surging from a chest wound. Chase instinctively grabbed Glenn and dragged him to the safety of a large bolder as other shots rang out, just missing both of them. Glenn's ashen face told Chase that he was fading fast. Chase looked at his friend as he tried to stop the bleeding.

"My notes," Glenn said between labored breaths.

"Don't speak, Glenn. Save your strength," said Chase as he tore an old rag in half. He dipped it in the cool stream and began packing it into the wound.

"There's something I need to tell you. Something you need to know." Glenn struggled to breath.

"Glenn, just hold on," Chase said as bullets ricocheted around them.

"My laptop—you have to get my laptop. Everything's…" Glenn coughed up blood again. "Everything's there…"

"Where? How? What's the password?" Chase was frantic.

"Under the seat of the pickup. Use fishin—" he coughed again and relaxed in Chase's arms.

Just then, a gun slid out of Glenn's side pocket. It was a Glock .45 caliber. Chase had only used a handgun once when he went shooting back in his college days. His power of recall heightened by the sound of footsteps and the adrenaline rush he was experiencing. He checked the magazine before flicking off the safety. Then he charged the weapon and crouched lower behind the rock. A man dressed in camouflage stepped around the corner of the boulder just enough for Chase to get a clean shot. He took aim and squeezed the trigger. The man fell back into the stream, his blood turning the crystal waters into a river of crimson. The man didn't move. Chase waited. No more shooting—just the sound of the water lapping over the rocks.

Chase had a big problem. He had two dead men, both of whom would not want their identities known.

Chase's cell phone vibrated.

"Chase, this is James Randall. Code word cakewalk."

Chase countered with the word, "Crosswalk."

"Mr. Vice President, are you all right? Are you in a safe place?" Chase said rather breathlessly.

"Yes, how about you?"

"No, as a matter of fact, I'm not. Are you familiar with the name Glenn Tibbits?"

There was a pause, "Yes, let me say I know of him," the vice president replied.

Chase's face tightened. "Well, he and I were out here in Colorado fishing, and a sniper just shot him. He died in my arms."

A moment of silence reigned. "Oh my…are you safe? Is your life in danger?" the vice president asked with rising concern in his voice.

"I was able to retrieve a handgun out of Glenn's pocket, and I got the drop on the guy. I shot him, and now I've got two dead guys lying here, and I don't know what to do next. I'm afraid that they may be looking for me, too. What should I do?" Chase paused to slow his breathing before continuing.

"Glenn said he had a laptop computer in his truck with information. Should I go and get it before someone else finds it?"

There was silence on the other end of the conversation as the vice president considered his answer. "Tell you what

I'd do. I'd wait until it gets dark, make my way back to the truck, and drive to town. The Sheriff of that town—what's his name?"

"Sheriff Conyers," Chase suggested.

"Yeah, Sheriff Conyers. He can be trusted, and he will handle this very quietly. Then you get your tail out of there and back to the safety of Washington, DC."

"Mr. Vice President, I don't think that will be much safer," Chase said as he wiped the sweat from his forehead and looked around.

"Just lie low until dark and get out of where you are as quietly as possible. I'll call you tomorrow at this same time and fill you in on what I know. Good-bye." With that, he hung up, leaving Chase to his thoughts. Chase closed his eyes and let his ears absorb the sound around him.

He let his mind drift to thoughts of Megan. He could see her face, smiling and innocent, and was glad she didn't know the predicament he was in. He momentarily considered calling her, but ruled it out for fear of making any noise or running the risk that her phone was tapped. Instead, he prayed for the Lord's protection for her and himself.

After waiting for what seemed an eternity, he decided to try to find his way to the truck. It was a moonless night, and the woods along the path leading from the river closed in like an unwelcome embrace. Chase made his way back to the truck as quietly as he could but not without stumbling several times on fallen logs and root outcroppings. He found the truck undisturbed and the laptop under the front seat. He opened it up and logged on using the password Glenn had given him. He scrolled around until he found what he was looking for. Pay dirt!

Chapter 6

Beaumont, Colorado...

Over the last two years since his retirement, Glenn had built an impressive file on all of the senators, members of the House of Representatives, the Judiciary, Cabinet appointments, and the twenty or so czars the previous president had made. There was evidence there that many of the key appointments were people who had links to the Order. Although the Order was exposed back four years earlier, it never was destroyed. It couldn't be. It was like an octopus; cut off one leg, and it had seven others that would wrap around you.

"So the Order is alive and well and back to its old tricks of infiltrating our country," Chase said to himself.

He placed the laptop back under the seat. Then he found a flashlight and carefully checked underneath the truck for a bomb. He found none. He pulled the key from the ashtray where Glenn left it and started the engine. Retracing the route back to the main road in the dark took time, and he got lost several times before finding his way to the paved road. It was past midnight when Chase got back to town.

As he entered the old jailhouse, Sheriff Conyers bolted to life. He was pulling a double shift and was sleeping deeply when Chase came in. His feet were propped up on the desk with the newspaper lying across his chest like a blanket. At the sound of the door opening and closing, he sat up so quickly that the chair nearly rolled out from under him.

Confusion was written all over the sheriff's face as he rubbed the sleep from his eyes. "Chase, what are you doing here and why are you covered in blood?" the sheriff said as he stood and greeted his friend.

Chase looked down at his blood-covered flannel shirt and then returned his gaze. "Hello to you too, Sheriff." The two friends shook hands as Conyers motioned him to take a seat.

"Sheriff, I've got a big problem, and I need your help."

"You don't say," the sheriff said as he eyed Chase wearily. "Who or what did you run into? By the looks of it, it was a chainsaw."

For the next thirty minutes, Chase unpacked the story of the vice president, the bug in Stan's office, and the shooting. Chase even showed the Sheriff what he found on Glenn's laptop. Conyers sat in silence, taking down the pertinent information.

He seemed to deliberate for a moment before he spoke. "Son, if what you're telling me is true," he paused and looked Chase directly in the eyes, "and I have no reason to doubt you, then we got a really big problem. First let me get you a clean set of clothes. I'll send out my most discreet deputy, and he will clean up the mess down at the river. In the meantime, you need to be high-tailing it out of here before you draw more attention to yourself."

Chase rubbed the back of his neck nervously, "What about my rented SUV and Glenn's pickup truck?"

"You and that laptop need to be in that SUV and driving, not flying, driving back to Washington, DC, pronto," the Sheriff said with an interesting glint in his eyes. "They may be looking for you at the airport, although I don't know why if they think the sniper did his job. But still you need to be driving."

Chase nodded and stood for a moment. "I think you're right about driving back. It might throw anyone who might be looking for me off the trail." He pulled out his wallet and checked his money.

"Just don't use your credit card for food or gas or anything. They might be able to track you that way. Here, here's some cash," Sheriff Conyers said as he pulled a wad of bills from his uniform shirt pocket. He handed the cash to Chase. "In the meantime, I'll be praying for you."

Chase looked with surprise at the Sheriff. "I didn't know you were a prayin' man."

Conyers looked up sheepishly, "I haven't been until a few years ago, but the new pastor at the Community First Church is a real believer, and he and I have become good friends. He took the time one day to show me from the Bible that I was a sinner, which I already knew I was. He showed me how I could have my sins forgiven. He took me to Colossians 1:13-14 and read, "Who hath delivered us from the power of darkness, and hath translated us into the kingdom of his dear Son: In whom we have redemption through his blood, even the forgiveness of sins.

"Chase, before I got saved, I lived a pretty sinful life. I did a lot of underhanded things to get and keep my job as sheriff, and I knew I needed God's forgiveness. The preacher showed me how by believing on the name of the

Lord Jesus Christ, I could know for sure that when I die I'll go to heaven. He showed me that if I committed just three sins a day, in a lifetime I would have accumulated over five hundred thousand sins. That convinced me that I needed to repent and turn to Christ. I trusted Him as my Savior, and man has that made a big, big difference in my life. Heck, we even have a Bible study going on right here in this jailhouse."

Chase let out a big laugh and slapped him on the back. "Man that's great. Megan and I have been praying that you would get saved. Praise the Lord!" There was a pause in the conversation, as neither knew what to say next.

"Well look, I had better be heading out of here," Chase said with a pained look on his face. "I sure feel bad about Glenn. He was one of the good guys." His voice trailed off and his eyes misted. "I hate leaving you with this mess."

Conyers inhaled and slowly exhaled to let the tension he was feeling subside. "Don't worry about it. I'll call my pastor, and we'll arrange a really nice funeral service for him and invite everyone. Glenn would have liked that. I do think, though, that before this is all over, a lot of good guys and bad guys are going to fall, too.

As he spoke, he walked to the corner of the jail, pulled out a box, and began rooting through it. He pulled out an old pair of blue jeans and a flannel shirt and tossed them to Chase. "Here, try these on."

Chase caught them and stepped into an empty cell and changed clothes. "They're a bit loose in the waist; could you take them in a bit?" he asked to lighten the mood.

The sheriff stifled a laugh at his friend's pun. "I don't know how you do it."

"Do what?" An innocent look crossed Chase's features.

Conyers shrugged his shoulders. "Keep your sense of humor after what you just went through."

Chase shook he head. "I guess it's the grace of God," he said with the palm of his hand outstretched.

The sheriff nodded his head, then scuffed the floor nervously. "Mind if we pray?"

"Sure, I'm going to need it," said Chase as he bowed his head.

After a short prayer, the two men shook hands and parted company. Neither thought that they would see each other alive again. Chase had lost a dear friend but found that he had gained a brother in Christ.

Chapter 7

Tuesday morning, Stan's Office

Stan sat behind his massive desk and thought about his situation. *I've got a bug in my office, so I can't talk freely. There is someone watching me. I can feel it, and I haven't heard from Chase in a couple of days. Megan is worried sick, and I can't tell her his whereabouts.* Suddenly his cell phone rang. He picked it up and looked at the caller ID. It was Chase. He checked his Doxa watch as he flipped open the phone. It was eleven a.m.

"Hello, Mr. Newberry, good to hear from you. It's been a while since we talked last."

Chase, who was rather confused, played along.

"Why don't you and I meet for lunch as soon as you get to town? How about at the Willard?"

Again Chase agreed.

"And by the way, I left you a Welcome to the Family packet down at the front desk. The Welcome to the Family packet is a pack of information including a new door pass key and badge for all new employees. When you get here, pick it up and look it over before you start your new job assignment."

Chase clearly didn't understand the melodrama but agreed to follow Stan's instructions.

"Okay, Mr. Berkowitz, I look forward to meeting with you and getting better acquainted. How about I come by tomorrow around this time?"

"Sure, that will be fine, Mr. Newberry. See you then." He hung up the phone and rubbed his forehead as a migraine set in.

Maybe, thought Stan, I should drive over to Chase's house and just tell Megan what is happening so she will stop worrying and stop calling me.

Stan stood, placed a pencil on the edge of his desk, and headed to his car on the parking level. He got in and turned the key. An explosion rocked the building. Flames engulfed the neighboring vehicles, and Stan was gone. The automatic sprinkler system came on, and by the time the fire and rescue squads arrived, the flames were under control. Stan's body was burned beyond recognition.

The early morning smog had not yet engulfed the city as Chase arrived back in Washington, DC. It was Wednesday morning, and Chase was road weary and hungry after driving nearly straight through. Rather than stopping by his house, he went directly to his office to inform Stan of the latest turn of events. He got to the office building on G Street to find yellow crime scene tape blocking off the parking level. He had to park a block away in another parking deck. Chase entered the lobby and approached the receptionist's deck on the first floor.

"What happened to the parking level?" asked Chase as he neared the receptionist.

She looked up as she fielded an inquisitive phone caller's questions, and for a moment, a glint of surprise came and went as she stared at Chase.

"Oh, Mr. Newton." Her eyes bore the pain she was feeling in her heart. "I guess you haven't heard. Mr. Berkowitz was killed yesterday by a car bomb!" She buried her face in her hands and wept uncontrollably.

Chase stood immobilized as he let the shock sink in.

"A car bomb!" he repeated. "How? Why?" Chase's mind was reeling.

It took several minutes before she could regain her composure. Finally she looked up, wiped her eyes, dabbed her nose, and tried to regain her composure.

"That's what everyone else has been asking, as well. The police have been all over this place, looking for evidence and asking a lot of questions."

The news of his friend's death left him shaken to the core. First it was Glenn, now Stan. Where was it going to end? Already feeling the effects of driving across the country, he was barely able to absorb the enormity of the situation. He was numb.

She was barely hanging on emotionally.

"When did this happen?" he asked as gently as he could.

"I don't know. Sometime around eleven thirty Tuesday morning."

That was about the time we had talked. Apparently, Stan decided to go somewhere after he talked with me, Chase thought to himself.

Choking down his emotions, Chase took a deep breath and steeled his nerves. "Is there a package for me?" he asked the receptionist.

"No, nothing for you," she replied absently.

He ran his hand through his hair and thought, What was it? There is something I'm missing. Then he remembered something Stan said. "Is there a Welcome to the Family packet, waiting to be picked up by a Mr. Newberry?"

The receptionist looked in the message center. "Oh, yes, there is one for Mr. Newberry. Would you like to have it?"

"Yes! Please." Chase took it and headed to his office, hoping, just hoping for no surprises.

A sigh of relief swept across the secretary pool as Chase stepped off the elevator. "Oh Mr. Newton, we were so worried for you," said one of the secretaries. "With you gone and Mr. Berkowitz dead, we didn't know what to do." She broke into sobs.

Chase leaned down and tried to console her. It was as much for his grief as it was for hers that the two embraced.

After grieving for several minutes over the loss of Stan, Chase regained control stepped into his office, and closed the door. He opened the Welcome to the Family packet, Chase emptied its contents on his desk. Rather than being new employee-related stuff, it was a message telling him to go to a location and follow their instructions. Under no circumstances was he to tell anyone, including Megan. Stan had written on a post-it that he was headed over to Chase's house to fill Megan in on the latest event.

So that's where he was going. That means M has no clue about what's been happening. She must be worried sick, he mused.

Chase looked around his office and wondered if it was bugged. He couldn't tell, and he wouldn't trust it not to be, so he left without calling his wife. He had a problem—how to get his wife up to speed on his latest assignment without compromising it.

Following the instructions left by Stan, Chase drove the rented SUV east on G Street to 11th Street, turned right, and headed north to the intersection of 11th and Clifton Street. He turned left and followed it until it dead-ended. The location indicated on the sheet of paper was a parking garage. He parked and stepped out of the vehicle.

The only door in the area that he could see led to a passageway. He followed it until it opened up to an alley. Cautiously, he started walking down a row of seedy looking shops. In nearly every doorway stood or leaned a rather unfriendly looking person. They were either guarding the door, or they were functioning as a lookout, but Chase couldn't tell which. As he approached one nasty-looking shop, the man in the doorway stepped into his path and unceremoniously ushered him in and closed the door. After looking through the blinds, he threw three or four dead bolts and flipped the "Open for Business" light off.

"You must be Mr. Newberry," the tattooed man said as he looked at the paper Chase was holding. "You're not very good at stealth, are you, Mr. Newberry?" his voice resonated in the small entry area.

By this time, Chase was getting the picture. "No, I guess I'm not," he said as he nervously tugged on his ear.

"Well in about an hour, you better get good and stealthy," the man said sharply, "or you'll be like poor, old

Stan. Now stand here and let me take some pictures of you and get your measurements. While I'm creating the new you, read this."

He handed Chase a dossier along with contacts and instructions on how Stan thought Chase should proceed. The instructions read like a Mission Impossible assignment, only there was no postlude saying that this document would self-destruct in ten seconds.

This was no TV show, this was a life and death struggle, and Chase was in the middle of it. Two of his dearest friends had just paid the ultimate price. He could be next.

The instructions he was to follow would put him in personal contact with James F. Randall and not just personal contact, but physical contact. He was to acquire a large enough sample of his DNA that the lab boys back at the tattoo shop, where he currently was, could analyze it. Then they would compare it with another DNA sample, one that they would get from the real James F. Randall. Finding, retrieving, and returning with that sample would prove to be the more dangerous of the two tasks. One slip up, and he would lead the enemy right to the vice president's hiding place.

How am I going to get that close to the president of the United States and make that kind of contact? He thought as he mulled over the possibilities.

The man with the tattoos returned with a full head mask, a wig, elevator shoes, and some body building material. "Okay, big boy, strip to the waist," he said as he pulled out a measuring tape.

Chase followed demurely as the man prepared to put the mask over his head. It was like Halloween, only scarier. By the time the man had finished, no one, not even himself, would have recognized Chase. He was taller, stronger looking, and much darker. In fact, he was now a member of a different race, and his new name was Cleve Newberry, MD.

Along with his new name came a complete identity change including a new job. Chase, aka Cleve, was now a medical doctor assigned to the president. His job was to monitor the president's physical condition on a daily basis and do a monthly physical examination. For that, Chase would need a crash course in the latest medical technology. The course included CPR and how to use an AED device, which is used to deliver a shock to the heart in the event that it has stopped. He also was trained on how to use a defibrillator. Chase was also instructed on taking someone's blood pressure, temperature, and how to draw blood. Chase had to learn all of these tasks and perform them as a professional, and he had to do it quickly. His credentials were already vetted, and he was expected on the job within the end of the week.

In the meantime, the current MD monitoring the president had been taken to the hospital with mysterious symptoms. He had cold sweats, the shakes, and a high fever. These were the results of a concoction administered to him by an FBI plant already working within the presidential medical detail. Chase's job would put him even closer than that operative could get. The plan also included the covert insertion of a witch's brew that would bring the president right to Cleve's medical facility before the president's monthly check-up came around. In essence, it was as close to an assassination attempt as one could get without actually killing the president.

For the next three days, Chase underwent intense medical training. By week's end, the man with tattoos on his arms and neck stepped into the room where Chase sat, crossed his muscular arms across his sizable chest, and asked, "Well, Cleve, what do yeah think?" with a big grin.

"I feel like a new man," Chase said as he viewed himself in a mirror. "By the way, you never told me your name. Who are you and who runs this operation?"

The big man looked down at Chase and shook his head slowly. "Always the reporter," he said with a smirk. "I can't tell you who runs this place or I'd have to shoot you but suffice it to say, we are the good guys. As for my name, why don't we keep it simple and call me Mr. Tattoo?"

Chase smiled at the cartoon image of the man. "It works for me."

"Good, you need to be because they are expecting you tomorrow morning at seven a.m. sharp," he said emphatically. "Come with your badge on and your medical kit in hand. Wear this stethoscope at all times, and I mean all times. In it is a TV monitor and listening device. Also you will be wearing an earpiece that looks like a Cochlear implant, but it's not. It's a mini microphone. We can speak to you any time we need to, and if you get into trouble, we have a medical team at the ready to talk you through most any crisis. You will also be monitored at all times by satellite and infrared heat sensors. You will never be out of our sight. Just don't lose those two items. If you do, you're on your own. Is that clear?" The man now sounded more like a drill sergeant than a common street vendor. Chase's blood pressure spiked.

"Sir yes, sir!" Cleve said enthusiastically. All he lacked was a "Hooah."

"Oh, by the way," said the man covered in tattoos as he studied Chase's eyes, "your wife is fine. Ever since you left to go fishing, Megan's cousin from Wisconsin has been visiting her and will see to it that she is cared for. So don't worry about her at all. Just focus on the task at hand."

Chase shook his head slowly. "What are you talking about? She doesn't have a cousin from Wisconsin."

"She does now, and they will get along just fine," he said, exposing a set of perfectly white teeth.

Pacified but not satisfied, Chase continued probing. "But why was I chosen for this job, anyway? I'm not an FBI agent."

"You are the only person that James Randall trusts and calls, so you are the go-to guy," he said with a smile, "so let's go save the country."

Chapter 8

A Week Earlier... Chase's House

Monday afternoon a week earlier there was a knock at Megan's door. She had not been expecting Chase so soon and had not gotten herself ready to greet him.

Maybe he got off work early, in that case maybe we could go out for a nice dinner and then a movie. But why would he be knocking? Megan thought to herself as she laid her laptop aside. Maybe he brought something home, and he has his hands full. *Whoever it is sure is insistent.* As she approached the front door, she had a funny feeling, a check in her spirit, that something was just not right. But because the knocking was nearly nonstop, she opened the door and was surprised by an enthusiastic bear hug.

"Megan, so good to see you. I've been so excited ever since I got on the plane, and now I'm here—your cousin from Wisconsin." With that, Linda Edwards stepped into Megan's house, dropped her suitcases and smiled.

Megan, not knowing what was going on, stood there incredulously. "But I don't have a cousin from Wisconsin."

"Oh, yes you do. I found you on the internet. I just did a people search, and there you were, my long lost cousin. I flew all the way from Milwaukee just to get reacquainted," she said with a big grin. "So don't just stand there, silly. Close the door, and let's get caught up. It's been years, and we have a lot to talk about."

With that, Megan obediently closed the door. As she turned around, she was met with a .45 caliber Rugar pointed at her face.

Without preamble, the woman looked into Megan's eyes. "Okay now, Megan, let's take this nice and easy. Come into the kitchen, and let's sit and talk."

Megan moved obediently as her heart pounded in her chest. She sat in one of the captain's chairs, and the woman claiming to be her cousin promptly duct-taped her arms to the arms of the chair.

"What is going on? Who are you, and what do you want?" Megan insisted as her frozen mind began to thaw out.

The woman didn't speak but rather drew out a syringe that was filled with a yellow fluid out of her purse. She held it pointed up, flicked it with her finger, and then inserted it in to Megan's left arm. A moment later, Megan was unconscious. Within minutes, Megan was un-taped, thrown over the shoulder of her kidnapper, and loaded into the trunk of her car. The kidnapper opened the garage door, backed out, and preceded down the driveway into the street and into the setting sun. As she drove through the subdivision, she passed a parked car with a woman sitting, or rather slumping, behind the wheel. The small hole left from the .22 caliber bullet was barely visible except for the trickle of blood, which ran down the side of her temple.

Megan woke up in a dark room with her hands handcuffed to the arms of an old, metal chair. Her mouth was duct taped, and she was slightly disoriented and nauseated from the drug. She could hear voices in the other room, but though she could speak several languages, they were not speaking in any language she understood. Then she heard someone stand up. The metal chair scraped the concrete floor and fell. Then a shadow approached the door and filled the entry with the bulging figure of a woman. She entered her room.

"Well, sleepy head, you finally decided to join the living?" a woman wearing a militia uniform said with a sneer.

Megan just stared at her with a burning anger.

"You will tell us where your husband is, or you will die. It's that simple."

Megan didn't know the whereabouts of her husband. He had left for work on Monday and a week later hadn't returned. She was as much in the dark as her captors. Stan wasn't much help, either; all he would say is that he was on assignment.

The woman tore the duct tape from her mouth, and Megan winced.

"You tell me where your husband is, and I'll not have to use this," she said as she pulled a .45 caliber Rugar out from behind her back.

The color drained from Megan's plaintive face. "I don't know where he is. His boss just said that he's on an assignment."

The woman charged her weapon and fired it in the air. Megan's ears rang with the deafening sound. She started to shake.

"Please, you must believe me. I don't know where he is," she pleaded.

Then the woman pointed the gun at her head. Megan closed her eyes, but just before she squeezed the trigger, the woman aimed the barrel above her head and fired again, singeing her hair from the flash of the weapon. By this time, Megan was in complete panic mode. Her mind froze, her muscles shook violently, and bile crept up her throat.

Suddenly, a man wearing a well-tailored suit and very expensive jewelry stepped into the room.

"What are you doing?" he said with a Russian accent. "Are you trying to kill our guest? Put that weapon away, and let's be hospitable." Then he reached down, unlocked the handcuffs that held Megan's hands, and handed her a bottle of water.

"Here, drink this." It was more of a command than a request.

Then he turned to the woman with the gun and dismissed her with a curse.

"Young lady, please forgive my subordinate. She has no class; she is just a peasant with a gun." He held out his hand. Megan recognized the man to be the Dean. She never knew his real name. All Megan ever heard him referred to was the nebulous title of "the Dean." He was the one who trained her father and who recommended him for the pastorate of the Community First Church in Beaumont, Colorado.

Many years earlier, the Dean, as he liked to be called, stepped on the stage of time. Only then he was the Dean of Religious Studies at Bruton College in Virginia. His primary focus was on Eastern Religions with an emphasis on yoga, spirit guides, and eastern mysticism. His mission was to recruit bright young people with leadership skills and bring them into the shadowy organization called the Order. His success rate was renowned. Before he came to Bruton, he had been in other institutions of higher learning. Over the past decades, his influence had reached as far as Oxford and Cambridge. He plied his trade at Cardiff University in Wales, Chalmers, in Sweden, Hasselt University in Belgium, Johannes Kepler University of Linz, Austria, Cairo University in Alexandria, Egypt, and Hellenic Open University in Athens, Greece. All of the great leaders of the Order had been at one time or another in his tutelage, and he held sway over their young impressionable minds. As it was then, so it was with one of his latest students, Pastor T.J. Richards.

Fear struck her heart as the memories of those last moments when she saw her father for who he really was flooded her mind.

This man is evil incarnate, she thought to herself.

He extended his hand and led Megan out of her cell into a brightly lit room where the other militiamen had been.

"Please sit here where it is more comfortable. Can I get you something? Food? Another bottle of water?"

Megan eyed him suspiciously and thanked him, yet refused.

"I have watched you for years, and now look at you. You have grown up to be a fine, young lady and a married one at that," he said with a whimsical look in his eyes. "Your father would be so proud of you. Well, on second thought, he might be disappointed with your choice of men to marry. Speaking of that, I'm sure you must miss your husband very much. I understand he had made a real name for himself ever since that unfortunate situation with the Document and such. The sooner you help us find your husband, the sooner you two can be together again."

Megan's eyes burned with anger at the mention of her father.

"But enough with reminiscing," he mused. Then his gray eyes grew suddenly cold. "We need some information that only you have. It would help us tremendously if you could provide us with it." His voice was soft and tender, but Megan could see in the line of his face that he was a man of steel.

Megan returned his gaze and forced a faint smile. "What kind of information?" Megan asked, knowing that whatever she knew would only be used against her husband and maybe her country.

The Dean looked at Megan. His eyes turned her blood to ice.

"We do need to get in touch with your husband most urgently. Could you call him on your cell phone and allow us to speak with him? I'm sure we could come to an amicable solution to this peccadillo," he said, his voice laced with sarcasm. It seemed to Megan that he was trying to put on a very good front in a very bad situation. He handed Megan her cell phone, and reluctantly she speed dialed Chase's number.

The prerecorded message said, "The customer you are attempting to reach is out of range, please try again later."

Chapter 9

Monday morning… The White House

Dr. Cleve Newberry stepped out of the limousine at exactly seven a.m. He strode confidently up to the guard-house and received a crisp salute, which he returned in like manner. He had spent the previous hours of the night reading his Bible and praying for Megan, himself, and the mission until God had given him peace, and assured him of His presence that he sought.

"Good morning, Dr. Newberry, you have been expected. We have a vehicle waiting for you. Please step this way. If you will follow Sgt. Hudson, he will escort you to the medical facility where you are assigned."

Dr. Newberry turned to the sergeant and followed him to a waiting golf cart. The ride was not that long, and the day was delightful. It reminded Chase of former days when he and his dad would spend a day on the golf course. They arrived at the back side of the White House and entered a restricted area. Chase couldn't help but notice the immaculately manicured lawn and shrubbery as he passed through the White House grounds.

"Just follow me, and I'll get you squared away in your office," the sergeant said crisply.

They left the golf cart behind and entered a corridor, which led to another corridor, which opened up to a row of doors. The third door on the right marked Medical Examiner was where they were headed. The sergeant opened the door and allowed Dr. Newberry to enter. "This is Nurse Hodges, and she will assist you from here. Have a wonderful day, sir." He turned crisply and walked back down the corridor.

Chase stood for a moment and watched the woman dressed in a nurse's uniform rise and approach him.

"Good morning, Dr. Newberry," Nurse Hodges said in a friendly tone. Then she extended her hand. "On behalf of the president, his family, and the White House staff, welcome!"

For an instant, there was a glimmer of recognition in Nurse Hodges eyes that sent a chill down Chase's spine, and then it was gone. For a moment, Chase forgot what he was doing in that place. He quickly regained his senses as a little voice in his earpiece made a wisecrack.

Chase tried to absorb her last statement. *I heard nothing about serving the first family and all the White House staff in this gig.*

"Well thank you for this warm welcome. I trust my services will be needed as little as possible."

"That's the best you can come up with?" he heard in his earpiece.

Chase cleared his throat.

Nurse Hodges shook her head in a womanly fashion.

"Oh on the contrary, your services will be quite in demand, as there is always someone coming down with something or getting hurt somehow. This is one of the busiest places in the White House," she said as she brushed a strand of hair out of her eyes.

Chase hesitated to answer too quickly and then scanned the room.

"Where is my examination room? I would like to get acclimated with everything."

Nurse Hodges moved with the finesse of a ballroom dancer as she led him into the adjoining room. It was set up pretty much the way his training room had been.

Chase put his hands on his hips and let out a slow whistle. "Good, this looks well lit and well equipped. I don't think that I'll need to requisition any new equipment," he said as he looked around.

Nurse Hodges nodded her head knowingly. "If you do need anything, just let me know, and I'll start the paperwork. We just might get it before the end of the president's term of office. Literally, it takes an act of congress to get something new around here."

Just then, the front door slammed, and Mr. Edwards, the chief of staff, walked into the examination room. His lips were tightly stretched across as set of pearly white teeth as he spoke with restrained anger.

"Nurse, why isn't there someone manning the reception desk? And why are you back here with the doctor? I'm sure Dr. Newberry has his hands full without you bothering him. Why don't you go back to your workspace and let me handle the good doctor?"

Mr. Edwards was a scheming little man with an attitude. Chase could see that the chief of staff was good at making enemies very quickly. His angular face and squinty eyes only accentuated his harsh personality. The intel that he was given was indeed accurate.

He squared himself directly in front of Chase and snapped, "Dr. Newberry, I don't know how you pulled it off, but you're here now, and as much as I don't like it, you and I are on the same team. But understand one thing. You will do nothing without my permission. I control access to the president! I control his schedule, and I will get you fired if I see you step out of line. Do you understand me?"

"Yep! Right on cue. Looks like Mr. Chief of Staff is the same as he's always been," said a voice in Chase's earpiece. Cleve scratched the back of his neck and replied respectfully, "Oh, yes, sir! Sir, is there anything else?" Chase said in his best accent.

The chief of staff looked rather shocked to be spoken to in that way. He turned on his heels and walked toward the door. Over his shoulder he said, "Pack up your gear and be at the back entrance. We leave in five minutes." With that, he stepped out of the examination room and was gone.

Chase poked his head out of the doorway and said with a mischievous grin, "How did I do?"

Nurse Hodges smiled back. "You did well for your first day on the job. Now let's get a move on. Grab your medical bag and follow me."

She was nearly in a run as she left the White House Medical Facility. Dr. Newberry was close on her heels.

"Where are we going?" he said between breaths.

"To the helo pad. It looks like the president is going somewhere, and wherever he goes, we go," she said as she reached the exit.

Outside the service entrance from where Chase had just come, a black Lincoln with flags on the front fenders awaited. The same sergeant that had just ushered him down the hallway now stood by the vehicle and was ready to close the door. He motioned for them to get in, and Dr. Newberry and his assistant slid into the car. The door closed behind them with a soft thud as they looked at each other.

"All set?" the driver asked and without a pause gunned the engine. Chase and Ms. Hodges were thrown backward into the plush seats. Within a few minutes, they were sitting at the helo pad, waiting to embark on an unknown journey.

The presidential entourage, including Chase and his medical team of one, loaded into the helicopter, and it lifted off the ground, sending grass clippings and dust into the cool morning air.

"Navy One to Air Force One, our ETA is ten minutes. Do you copy?" said the pilot of the helicopter in monotone syllables.

"Copy that, Navy One. See you in ten. Over and out."

Ten minutes later, the helicopter touched down yards away from a massive airplane with "Air Force One" painted on the tail fin. The president, followed by his personal staff, disembarked the helicopter and made their way up the stairway to the plane followed by the press corps. It seemed a bit funny to see his colleagues sitting back in the area designated for the press while he and the presidential delegation sat in much more comfortable seats.

After takeoff, the captain turned off the seat belt light and announced that they were allowed to move about the cabin.

"Dr. Newberry," Chase heard his nurse behind him. It took a moment to realize that she was speaking to him. "Dr. Newberry, would you follow me? I will take you to the medical facility on board Air Force One." He gave her a questioning look and stood up to follow. For the moment, was enjoying his new position in life.

The medical department was located one floor down from the main flight deck. It was a complete medical clinic; everything he needed was at his fingertips. He just hoped he didn't need to use them.

"Do you know where we are going?" Chase asked the nurse as he scanned the room.

Nurse Hodges nodded. "Yes, they briefed us yesterday. We are headed to Somalia. The president will be attending a conference on global warming. He was invited by the Somalian government to join them in a signing ceremony. The two nations are some of the last countries not to have signed the United Nations Framework Convention on Climate Change, known around the White House as the UNFCCC; they plan to sign it as a joint venture. He'll be making a speech and is expected to sign the Kyoto Protocol Treaty as well. The treaty was designed by the United Nations with the goal of controlling the amount of greenhouse gases that are released into the atmosphere," she said instructively. "If you ask me, the effects of that treaty will just about destroy our economy and intrude upon our sovereignty as a nation. I wish he wouldn't sign it."

"Sorry about that, chief," Chase heard in his earpiece.

"Great, I wish I knew about this before today. I would have brought my suntan lotion," Chase said with a wry smile.

His assistant shrugged her shoulders nonchalantly. "Don't worry, Doctor." She reached out and squeezed his hand. "We won't be out in the sun too much."

Chase nodded, stepped behind his desk, and sat down.

What is it about Nurse Hodges that reminds me of somebody else? Was it the way she spoke? Or the way she squeezed my hand? He sat in thought for a moment before Mr. Edwards barged into his office and interrupted his thoughts.

"Dr. Newberry, the president has asked to see you in the presidential suite, immediately, so drop what you are doing and follow me. Listen carefully to my instructions. You'll say, 'Yes, Mr. President,' 'No, Mr. President.' Do you understand me?"

Chase could hardly keep from laughing, but he contained himself as replied soberly, "Yes, sir!" he mumbled.

In return, Edwards shot him a look of steel, ice, and fire. The two men arrived at the door or the presidential suite. Two large Marines in dress uniform flanked it. The chief of staff knocked lightly, and a voice from within said, "Enter."

The chief of staff opened the door and stepped in followed by Chase.

"Sir, this is Dr. Cleve Newberry, your Chief Medical Examiner."

"Thank you, Mr. Edwards. That will be all." The president reached out his hand and shook Chase's.

"Dr. Newberry, it's a pleasure to meet you. Please take a seat. You never know when this plane might hit an air pocket," said the president as he assessed the doctor.

Chase nervously took his seat and glanced around the miniature version of the Oval Office. On the carpeted floor was the presidential seal, and the United States flag stood behind the desk. Chase's trained eyes began studying the president's mannerisms as he began to relax in his cushioned seat. He had interviewed Randall on numerous occasions and had noticed several idiosyncrasies about him. In the past interviews, he noticed that the vice president had a habit of touching his fingers to the top of the desk as he spoke. It was a small movement often used to emphasis an important point but was one that he repeated. Chase watched as the president as he spoke; not once did he touch the top of the desk. Chase made a mental note of the subtle change.

The president's next statement captured Chase's attention again. "Dr. Newberry, I noticed in your records that you are a navy man. You served on the USS Theodore Roosevelt and saw a bit of action during Operation Desert Storm in 1991." The president's blue eyes had a searching, probing look in them.

Chase nodded slightly. "Yes, sir. I was a much younger man back then."

The president's expression didn't change as he continued. "That was before David Architzel assumed command of the USS Theodore Roosevelt, wasn't it?"

"Yes, sir. I served under David J. Venlet," he said, having memorized his dossier thoroughly.

The president opened a folder and glanced down at a few scribbled notes. "I also see here that you were awarded the navy and marine corps medal for sea rescues involving risking your life."

To that Chase smiled. "Yes, sir, and I would do it again if I had to."

The president considered his last statement for a moment.

"Well, Dr. Newberry, it is good to have you on board my team. I am told that I am scheduled to come to your office next week for a check up."

Chase hesitated, not wanting to sound too eager. "Yes, sir, and I look forward to giving you a clean bill of health."

After having concluded his brief interview, the president smiled and rose to his feet. Again he extended his hand, and the two men shook hands firmly.

"Thank you, Doctor. That will be all for this time. Have a nice flight. Oh, and be sure to stop by the executive dining room and order the biggest steak we have on board. Tell them it's on the house, compliments of the president."

Mr. Edwards, the chief of staff, stepped back in the presidential suite and ushered Chase out.

"That will be all, Doctor. They need you back in the clinic, so you had better get a move on," he snapped.

Chase reentered the medical clinic and found a Secret Service agent bleeding from the nose.

"What happened to you? Did you get into a fight with a door jamb?"

The agent nodded. "Yes, sir. That last air pocket we hit sent me right into the bulkhead, and wham-o, to the moon," he said as he lightly touched the purple wound on his nose and upper lip.

"Relax, Chase, this is routine stuff," said the voice in his earpiece. "Just apply pressure on the pressure point under his jaw and put a roll of gauze up under his front lip. Tell him to hold his head back, and that should stop the bleeding."

Chase followed the instructions, and, to his surprise, it worked. His first patient survived. Chase felt great.

The flight, which took ten hours, gave Chase a chance to rest, read, and administer a few bandages before arriving at its destination. After his last patient, who was suffering from a stomach virus, the pilot's voice came over the intercom, instructing everyone to prepare to land.

The giant plane landed in Mogadishu, the capitol, at around ten a.m. Sunday morning and was taxied to a halt near a small building that served as the airport terminal. A set of stairs was rolled out to the side of the plane followed by a large roll of red carpet. Then a military detail marched briskly up to the carpet and took their positions along either side of it. A heavily decorated four-star general proceeded to the top of the stairs and saluted the president as he deplaned.

At the bottom of the stairs awaited the presidential limousine and several more Lincoln Town Cars. The presidential detail loaded up in their respective vehicles and departed, heading for the presidential palace. The lead car was filled with Secret Service personnel, the second car was a decoy, and the third car held the president, and Dr. Newberry was assigned to the fifth car back. Following them was another vehicle with Secret Service personnel and then the press corps.

As Chase stepped out of the shadow of the massive aircraft, he was greeted by a blast of acrid, dry air. The temperature must have been 110 degrees in the shade.

His first breath nearly seared his lungs, and he wondered how anyone could exist in such an extreme environment. He placed a new pair of Izod Polaroid sunglasses on his face and hoped the heat wouldn't deteriorate his disguise. Fortunately he was only exposed to the brutal heat for the few moments it took to descend the stairs and enter the waiting Lincoln Town Car. By then, however, he was sweating profusely, as was his nurse. He settled into his seat, buckled the seat belt and looked around at the stark scenery.

"This sure is a lot hotter than I ever imagined. Maybe next time we can land somewhere in Antarctica," Chase said as he mopped his brow with a handkerchief.

Nurse Hodges just smiled and brushed the hair behind her ear. A look of concern filled her face. She was clearly uncomfortable with her current circumstance.

The motorcade pulled out and left the confines of the airport. It wormed its way along the pothole-ridden highway until it neared a population center. The houses and people closed in, and Chase suddenly felt claustrophobic.

Chapter 10

The Streets of Mogadishu…

Chase was not prepared for what was about to happen, but his survival instincts took over when his brain failed him. The lead vehicle suddenly jolted into an upright position as the IED, Improvised Electronic Device, exploded underneath it. The car flew into the air and landed upside down on the second car. Immediately, the air was filled with gunfire as the ambush ensued. It was as if someone had kicked a beehive the way the bullets swarmed around each of the stalled vehicles.

The president's car came under fire as the insurgents took aim on it. Quickly, the other vehicle with Secret Service agents pulled alongside the president's car and gave it cover on the right side. The car Chase was in pulled alongside on the left. They had come to a stand still for the moment as the head of security assessed the situation.

"Incoming!" screamed the chief of staff as an RPG, a rocket-propelled grenade, struck just in front of the presidential vehicle. The explosion tore through the windshield, killing the driver instantly. The president exited the burning vehicle and took cover between cars. In the face of a withering barrage of bullets, Chase jumped from the relative safety of his vehicle, grabbed the president by the arm and dragged him back into his car.

"Mr. President, are you all right?" Chase asked as he noticed him hold his side. The answer was obvious. Blood was seeping through the president's shirt. Nurse Hodges grabbed his medical kit and began to pull packing material from it and handed it to Chase.

"Pack the wounds. We have to stop the bleeding," said the voice in his earpiece. Chase acted quickly with what little trauma training he had.

Chase took the president's face in his hands and spoke directly to him, "Mr. President, can you breathe all right?"

"Yes, but I think a piece of shrapnel pierced my bullet-proof vest."

With trembling fingers, Chase ripped open the president's shirt only to find a bulletproof vest protecting the man's upper body. He released the Velcro that held it in place and removed it just long enough to find the wound.

Sweat beaded on Chase's upper lip as he realized the gravity of the situation. The very man he was sent to expose as an imposter was now handed the responsibility of saving him from certain death. Chase fished his finger in the wound. "There it is. We have to get that thing out without it doing any more damage."

The area of the wound was on the lower left of the abdomen, and to the best of his knowledge, there were no vital organs in the immediate area. Chase felt around the area of the entry wound, took a calculated guess, and found the end of the shrapnel. Fortunately, the bulletproof vest blunted most of the impact, and the piece of metal had only punctured the abdominal wall. Chase removed the piece and began packing the wound.

Outside the car, the battle continued with no sign of abating. Several Secret Service agents had been wounded and were lying where they fell. With the president's condition under control, Nurse Hodges jumped from the car and attended to one of the fallen men. Chase knew that if they didn't get out of this situation fast, all would be lost. He made a radical decision. The driver of his vehicle had exited the car and was returning fire. Chase jumped over the front seat, slammed it in reverse, and sped backward. Just then, another RPG hit the ground nearby, leaving a gaping hole. He did a 180-degree turn and headed back to the safety of the airport and prayed that Air Force One was not doing the usual practice touch-and-go exercises. As it turned out, the plane had not had time to taxi out and take off, but was still in the same position as it was when they left it.

Chase made a beeline to the stairway and screeched to a halt. The security detail protecting Air Force One had already taken up positions when the head of the security detail called in the attack.

"Mr. President," Chase said breathlessly, "can you make it out of the car?" As he jumped out and came around to the side of the car where the president sat holding his side, a pained expression registered on the president's face.

"Yes, but I'll need some help up those steps."

Chase put the president's right arm over his shoulder and guided him up the stairs while other staff members came alongside to help them. Once Chase got the president squared away, he turned to leave.

The president looked up from the gurney he was lying on. "Where are you going, son?" he said with an expression of true concern on his face.

Chase paused at the bulkhead and turned. "Look, Mr. President," the lines in his eyes etched in worry, "I left my nurse on the ground helping with the wounded, and I'm not leaving her."

The president looked at Chase thoughtfully. "Son, this plane is leaving immediately, and if you're not on it, you'll be left behind," he said flatly.

"Well, so be it. I'm not going to let an unarmed lady fall into the hands of that angry mob." He stepped off the plane.

In his earpiece he could hear Mr. Tattoo saying, "The mission, don't forget the mission."

"Forget the mission. I'm not leaving Ms. Hodges to a pack of angry wolves," he said as he descended the stairs and climbed back into the shot-up Lincoln Town Car. He slammed the door shut, put the car in gear, and sped back into harm's way.

As the battle continued, more Somalians descended on the beleaguered security detail. It would only be a matter of time before they were overwhelmed.

Chase pulled up to the encircled cars, jumped out and grabbed one of the wounded men. Nurse Hodges grabbed another and dragged him to the car. One of the remaining Secret Service agents followed suit by taking the chief of staff by the arms and literally tossing him into the waiting vehicle. The remaining detail all piled in as Chase jammed the car back in reverse and repeated the trip.

At some point in time, Chase realized that someone was screaming in his earpiece. His back-up team was trying to get his attention, but with all of the explosions and gunfire, it was hard to hear. By the time Chase could give it any attention, most of the danger was behind him. He chose to ignore whoever was screaming at him. As he approached the airport, he saw Air Force One lifting its nose skyward. Chase's heart sunk like a rock.

Oh no! he thought. *We're stranded in a foreign country full of angry, America-hating people with no way out!*

"Look, Doctor," said one of the agents. "There's a C17 getting ready to take off. It's one of our support planes, and it maybe our only hope of getting out of here."

The rear ramp was still down as if it was the jaw of a hungry alligator. "If I can catch up to that plane, maybe I can drive this car right up the ramp before it lifts off," Chase announced with a look of determination in his eyes.

An agent leaned over the front seat. "It's risky, but what are our chances if we hang around this dump?" he said as he watched a caravan of jeeps and SUVs loaded with gun-toting Somalians giving chase.

Chase spun the car around and headed in the direction of the C17. By the time he got near the plane, it had accelerated to 100 miles an hour, and Chase had to hold it steady to get through the jet wash. With the ramp still down, sparks flew up and hit his windshield as it scraped along the tarmac. Chase nosed the car directly behind the mammoth airplane and gunned the engine. It lunged forward, hit the edge of the ramp, bounced, and raced up the ramp. Were it not for the cargo netting, the car would have driven out of control right into the flight deck. The netting held, and the car slammed to a halt. Just as it came to rest, the bay door closed, and the mighty plane rose into the air. A cheer went up from the flight crew but went unnoticed by Chase and those in the car.

"Man, that was close. Everybody okay?" Chase asked as he looked around the passenger compartment of the car.

"Sir, we've got two wounded, one KIA, and three able-bodied people on board," said his nurse.

A look of deep concern crossed Chase's face at the mention of someone being killed in action. With an extra effort of willpower, he asked, "Who is the KIA?"

There was a pause before she spoke. "It's Mr. Edwards, the chief of staff," Nurse Hodges said softly.

Their eyes met as each read the other's thoughts.

"That's too bad. I didn't even have a chance to tell him about the Lord," Chase said with true sorrow in his heart.

A moment of silence passed.

"The rest of you are okay?" Chase asked, looking at his nurse for conformation.

"A bit shaken up, but we'll make it. Thanks for coming back to get us. If you didn't, we'd all be dead by now," said one agent as he patted him on the shoulder.

"Yes, sir, Doc! All but one of us were out of ammo. If you hadn't returned when you did, we wouldn't have made it. We all owe you our lives. Thank you!" said another one of the security detail. There was a crackling of static in his earpiece, and then he heard the cheers of his comrades back home.

Chapter 11

Hidden Somewhere in DC

Vice President Randall tried his cell phone again only to get the same results. "The party you are attempting to reach is out of range."

For the first time, Randall began to worry. The only man who could prove his identity could very well be dead, or so he thought.

He and his only bodyguard had found a safe place to hide, but it would only be a matter of time before someone discovered his whereabouts and called the people who sought his life. He had to keep moving, but the more he moved, the greater the chance was that they would pick up his trail. Really there was only one place to hide where they would not think of looking, but getting there was a problem. Keeping it a secret was even a bigger problem.

How did this happen? the vice president thought to himself. *How could this have taken place? The best-informed, best-protected, best-insulated men in the world were ambushed simultaneously. This could only have happened with a lot of insider information. It is obvious that there are moles in our administration. But they all couldn't be traitors. Surely someone loyal to the president would have stepped forward and let the chief of security know about a plot to assassinate the president and vice president. Maybe that explains why several of the members of my security detail suddenly turned up missing last week,* he surmised.

The vice president let his mind wander back to the days early in the presidency. President Donovan had won a landslide victory over the liberal democrat challenger, and his coattails swept in a majority of his colleagues. It looked like they had a mandate to implement many of the sweeping reforms that he (they) had promised on the campaign trail. All that changed in a moment. All that they worked for now hung by a thread, and even that was showing signs of strain.

In the short time that he had been in office, the new president, the most liberal of his party, had taken steps to liberalize trade agreements with countries that were known for harboring terrorists and were guilty of human rights violations. At the same time he snubbed those countries who had been our friends and allies down through the years.

If the signing of the Kyoto Treaty is enacted, Vice President Randall knew he had an uphill climb to turn things around if he ever got back into office. The stakes were high, and the risks were even higher.

Washington, DC...

The room where Megan was being held was intentionally cold; the thin garment she was wearing when she was abducted didn't do much to keep out the chill. The fact that she was gripped with fear didn't help the situation, either. With her arms and hands handcuffed to an old, rusty, metal chair, she had little maneuverability, and she was getting numb from her bottom up. Her cell phone lay on the table. All she had to do was call her husband, and her captors would do the rest. She couldn't do it. It wasn't that she hadn't tried—nothing would bring her more comfort than to hear her husband's voice—but every time she called, she got the same message; "The party you are trying to reach is out of range."

After all that we have been through, did it all have to come down to this? Megan let her mind drift back to the time when they first met, more than five years ago. Her first recollection of seeing Chase was when she barged into his dusty office in the *Beaumont Observer* and asked him if he would help her learn the journalism business. She was the editor of her junior college's newspaper, and he was a cub reporter. He was the kind of guy who thought he knew it all, and he had a reputation for demonstrating it. She obviously didn't make a big impression on him the first time they met. Either that or maybe he already had a girlfriend; she couldn't tell. But Megan was used to getting her way. The second time she saw him, she tried to make a bigger impression. Her attempt at running him over in the crosswalk definitely got his attention. She smiled at the thought, handcuffed to the chair. Chase claimed it was that silly, impulsive act that got the whole series of events started. It ended in her becoming a multi-millionaire and the wife of Mr. Chase Newton.

How could these people be the same evil people that she and Chase exposed? I thought that the Order was defeated. Why was this evil man who called himself the Dean involved in abducting me? And why do they want my husband?

The only thing she could think of was that they wanted revenge.

Megan prayed.

Chapter 12

Beaumont, Colorado

Sheriff Conyers made all the arrangements for the funeral for Friday afternoon. He called on his pastor, the new pastor of the Community First Church, to lead a funeral with an emphasis on worship and celebration. Since Pastor T.J.'s disappearance, the church was left with only a few remaining members and an open pulpit. The pulpit committee moved quickly to fill the vacancy—only they spent much more time praying rather than reading resumes. God led a very godly young man to the church, and he proved to be just what the hurting, beleaguered church needed.

Pastor Steve Callahan was anxious to establish a strong witness for Christ in that part of Colorado. He was prayerful and fervent, a real man of the Word. His zeal brought him to Sheriff Conyers' jail, where he led several detainees to the Lord. That's how the sheriff heard the gospel, as well. His conversion affected the whole way he ran the police department. No more informants and no more under the table deals. From then on Sheriff Conyers was an honest broker. The change that Christ made in his life was immeasurable, and the whole community took notice of it. So when the death of Glenn Tibbits was announced from the pulpit of the Community First Church, many people called for Sheriff Conyers to take the lead in making the funeral arrangements.

Once again the church was packed as friends, and well-wishers came from miles around to give their last respects to a man who embodied godliness.

Pastor Callahan opened the service with a simple prayer followed by a brief eulogy. Rather than having a soloist sing, the sheriff asked the organist to play an old favorite, and the congregation sang along. Pastor Callahan read from John 11:25. "Jesus said unto her, I am the resurrection, and the life: he that believeth in me though he were dead, yet shall he live."

Then he turned his attention to the grieving assembly and spoke encouragingly, "Friends of Glenn Tibbits, we are here to celebrate the home-going of a dear saint of God. The bodily form of Glenn remains, but he is alive and well in heaven with Christ his Savior. That happened the moment Glenn's heart stopped and he took his first breath of heavenly air. Though we grieve his passing, we grieve mostly for our loss not his gain. But if Glenn was to return and give us one message, I would say that he would tell his unsaved friends this, 'Prepare to meet thy God,' from Amos chapter four verse twelve." He allowed time for his words to sink in before pressing on.

"Friends, one of these days, all of us will die, and it is in this life that we must prepare for that day. Do like Glenn did a few years ago when he acknowledged to God that he was a sinner in need of a Savior, and he placed his faith in the finished work of Christ to get him to heaven. That was how he made his preparations by putting his trust in the Lord Jesus Christ. We are not guaranteed tomorrow. You can trust Christ where you sit. Don't delay."

He paused long enough to shift gears. "For the believer, Glenn would say the same thing—prepare. Live every day as if it were your last. Live it fully and wholeheartedly for the Lord. There is no such thing as wasted time when it is spent in prayer, Bible reading and study, and in sharing your faith. Then when it's all said and done, you, too, will have a great sendoff celebration like the one being held down here and a great celebration in heaven. For the Bible says, 'Precious in the sight of the Lord is the death of his saints,' in Psalm 116:15."

The pastor smiled, closed his Bible, and stepped down from the pulpit and asked the congregation for testimonies from those who knew him best. An hour later the line of friends extended down the main aisle as people waited to say a good word on behalf of Glenn Tibbits. But as the hour was getting late, the pastor gently closed the testimonial time and led the processional out of the sanctuary and held a brief graveside committal service.

When Sheriff Conyers returned to his office in the front of the jailhouse, a copy of the *New York Times* was laying on his desk. Since two of his dearest friends ran the paper, the least he could do was to subscribe to it and read it. Most of the time, he enjoyed the commentaries and editorials. This time what he read made his blood boil.

The front page read, "*New York Times* Editor Stan Berkowitz dies in car bombing." How could this be? Both of his friends died violent deaths. The sheriff knew only what Chase told him, and he knew enough to get himself killed. So why sit here in Colorado and wait? I have to do something, and I have to do something now.

Sheriff Conyers fueled his police cruiser and prepared to drive to Washington, DC, leaving the jail in the hands of his deputies. He packed lightly, but he packed heat—a lot of it; he had with him a couple of handguns, a shotgun, and enough ammunition to start or end a war. But before he left town, he made one last stop. He went over to the pastor's house and asked him to get the prayer chain started.

Sheriff Conyers kicked the ground nervously as he tried to think of the right words to say.

"Brother Callahan, I am leaving on very important police business, and it would mean a lot to me if I knew that you and the church family were praying for me. I believe that there will be some danger involved, and I need God's protection and providential guidance. Would you do that for me?"

A bright smiled broke across the pastor's face. "Sheriff, it would be a privilege to be your prayer support. Why don't we pray right now before you go?" The two men prayed, and the sheriff left within the hour.

An hour later a black sedan slowly drove through town. The driver had one thought on his mind.

Where is Sheriff Conyers?

Chapter 13

Thirty Thousand Feet over Africa

The C17 leveled off at 30,000 feet, and the occupants of the Lincoln Town Car climbed out and stretched.

Nurse Hodges had pieces of glass in her hair, and smudges of Somalian dirt obscured the lovely features of her face. Chase, on the other hand, was no worse for wear save for the blood-soaked shirt he wore. He was checking his disguise in a mirror as one of the security agents interrupted his thoughts.

"Sir, we have wounded who need your attention," said one of the security detail. Chase grabbed his medical kit and stepped over the cargo netting to a wounded man and knelt down. Nurse Hodges came to his side and handed him his stethoscope.

"You dropped this when you climbed over the car seat," she said with an interesting glint in her eye.

"Thank you, Nurse. I don't know what I'd do without this—or you for that matter." Then he turned his attention to the dying man.

The young man's shirt was soaked with blood, and he was already unconscious from the loss of blood. He had several entry wounds, and by the time he was extracted from the battle zone, he was past saving. The voice in his earpiece confirmed what he already knew. Chase moved to the other wounded man. His wounds were not as life-threatening. The medical backup team talked him through how to treat his wounds and stop the bleeding. Chase felt good that in some small way he had made a difference.

As Chase stood and steadied himself, one of the able-bodied security agents stepped up. "Sir, it's going on noon and we are about an hour behind Air Force One. They are headed to Ramstein Air Base, one of two fully operational air bases left in Germany."

Chase rubbed the back of his neck and looked at the man, "How long before we get there?"

He paused and did some quick calculation. "We should get there in about fifty minutes," he said without explanation.

Chase nodded and flexed his fingers, realizing that he had strained his hand when he rescued the president. Suddenly weariness settled over him like a wet blanket. It was the aftermath of an adrenaline rush, and he needed to sit down. As he walked over to the side of the car, he said to himself and to the ever-listening support team back in Washington, "Well, I guess I failed."

Not knowing who he was talking to, Nurse Hodges responded, "What do you mean you failed?" She had been sitting in the car, attempting to rest when Chase leaned against the car.

"You didn't fail. You were rather heroic in my book," she said as she brushed the hair out of her eyes. "You saved the president's life and the remaining security detail from certain death. I'd say that was a pretty good day of work."

He shrugged and looked uncomfortable. "Yes, well, I still feel that I could have done more. Look, I'm covered in the president's blood and who knows what else," Chase said as he looked at his shirt and slacks.

"Well, if it means something, I did get this," Nurse Hodges said as she pulled a vial of blood from her pocket.

Chase froze and stared at the tube of blood like a hungry vampire. "What is it? Or rather whose is it?" he said as he eyed the tube.

A bright smile crossed her face. "It's the president's. While you were extracting the shrapnel, I was taking a blood sample. He never even noticed," she said with a conspiratorial tone.

Chase tried to suppress a grin. "How? I mean, why? I mean…"

She looked at him with an impish twinkle in her eyes.

"Let's just say we might need it for future reference and leave it at that," she said ruefully as she pressed the tube into his hand and squeezed it.

How strange, Chase thought. What is it about her that reminds me of someone else, someone who squeezed my hand the same way?

Chase sat in the back seat of the car and closed his eyes. He began to pray for Megan and his friends back in Washington. His mind wandered back five and a half years to the early days of when he and Megan realized they loved each other. The time spent in the coffee shop had become more than just a time to talk. It had become a time to share their secrets and dreams. Soon their hearts knit as one. It was in Maxine's Diner that Chase asked Megan to marry him. When she said yes, everyone in the diner cheered.

Because of the rapid pace of Chase's life after the ordeal involving the Order, the marriage planning was pretty simple. A guest preacher was brought in, and the sanctuary was decorated with flowers from the only flower shop in town. What few church members were still left and the town's people nearly filled the auditorium to witness the ceremony. After the wedding they had a four-course banquet catered by none other than Maxine's Diner. It was a wonderful ending to an exciting chapter in both of their lives—and a wonderful beginning to a new chapter.

Now Chase wondered if Megan ever learned of his assignment and if her life was in danger.

Chase's cell phone vibrated. He looked down at the caller ID; it was Vice President Randall.

"Chase, are you all right?" his resonate voice carried a deep sense of concern. Chase sat up and cleared his throat. "Yes, sir, I am, albeit a bit shaken up."

For a moment static filled his phone. "I've been trying to reach you for days! Where are you? Are you safe? Is this a good time to talk? I can hardly hear over that roaring sound. What is it?" asked the vise president with tension growing in his voice.

Chase looked around the interior of the mammoth aircraft and decided to talk over the noise. "To start with," he said, "the president's motorcade came under attack in Mogadishu, and the president was wounded."

The vice president took a sharp breath. "Is he all right? I mean, did he survive?"

Chase replayed the conflict in his mind's eye. "Yes, well, an RPG hit the presidential car, and he was wounded. I was able to get the shrapnel out and stop the bleeding before he lost consciousness. He will make it. I got him back on Air Force One, and they took off headed for Ramstein Air Force Base in Germany." He paused to take a swig from a bottle of water. "I left the plane and went back to get the rest of his protective detail. They were still battling it out with the Somalians when I arrived. It's a good thing I got there when I did too. They were just about to be overrun. They piled in the car I was driving, and we high-tailed it out of there. Then we caught the C17 on the run. We are now about thirty thousand feet in the air and about forty-five minutes behind Air Force One. I am safe, but this is not a good time to talk. I don't know who I can trust."

Again static filled the phone as the signal passed through some interference. "I had no idea," said the vice president. There was an uncomfortable pause in the conversation as each man absorbed the gravity of the situation.

Then the vice president spoke softly. "Thank God you were there for the president. I shudder to think what would have happened if he died, even if he is an imposter."

Chase exhaled slowly to keep the tension from taking over, "How about you, Mr. Vice President? Are you in a safe place?" inquired Chase as he looked to see if anyone was listening.

The vice president waited a moment to collect his thoughts before proceeding. "I'd rather not disclose my whereabouts just yet. You never know who might be picking up this phone call. I fear I may have endangered your life," the vice president admitted. "I'm so sorry for what I've put you through. Maybe I should just turn myself in and face the consequences."

"The consequences?" Chase asked vehemently. "The consequences would be your death, and I'm not about to let that happen—not after what I've just been through. Look, you need to stay the course, Mr. Vice President. You need to ride this one out. We're not out of the game, yet. Just remember that the fat lady hasn't sung until I say, 'Sing.' Okay?" Chase spoke with a lot more bravado than he was feeling.

Randall was surprised by the confidence that exuded from the voice on the other end of the phone connection.

"Well, you are right. I was just feeling sorry for myself more than for you," said the crest-fallen vice president. "I'll continue my game of hide and seek down here, and you keep up the good work on your end, son. Now I had better get off the phone. I'll call you again in a day or two. Good-bye."

Chase looked at his stethoscope. "Did you guys hear that? Did you get a trace on the origin of the call?" he asked softly to the guys back in Washington, DC.

"Yeah, we heard it, but we don't have that kind of technology to trace that type of call," Mr. Tattoo admitted.

"Did you hear that Nurse Hodges got a blood sample?" he continued.

The connection crackled as the plane bounced through the tips of some cumulus clouds. "Yes, and that is great news. Now we need that sample analyzed as soon as possible," said the voice on the other side of the world.

Chase smiled and glanced down at his nurse. "We are about to land at Ramstein Air Force Base, and the president may be asking for me."

Mr. Tattoo picked up the narrative. "Our intel says he has already landed, picked up another medical team, and is in route for the United States as we speak."

Chase glanced at Nurse Hodges. "So what are we supposed to do? Wait in Germany or catch the first flight out?" inquired Chase as he gestured with his hand.

There was a moment's pause as Mr. Tattoo conferred with his team.

"No, we need that analysis done there in our lab in Germany," he said flatly.

Chase sat up in his seat. "You guys have a lab over here?" he asked with a raised eyebrow.

"We are a branch of the FBI, and we have a field office with a state-of-the-art lab in many countries. Those boys in Germany can be trusted. Now listen carefully as I tell you where to go and who to contact. It won't be a straight line, so listen. Go to the motor pool and commandeer a vehicle. You have enough pull as head of the presidential medical team to be able to do that. Then you and your team go to Haus des Burger Stadium and go to ticketing. Ask for your 'will call' tickets and go to those seats."

Chase stood and began pacing; he was amazed at how quickly a back-up plan had been assembled. "You said team and tickets. There is only one of me." Chase asked looking around the wide body of the airplane.

"You will need the assistance of Nurse Hodges if you are to pull this off and survive. When in doubt, follow her lead."

Chase stopped pacing and looked across to the other side of the car at his nurse and nodded. "Yes, sir!"

The C17 did a perfect three-point landing and taxied up to the terminal. Before Chase and the others could get themselves unstrapped, members of the military from Ramstein's Air Force Base assembled at the bottom of the portable stairs. The commanding general and many of his staff gathered to express their gratitude to Dr. Newberry for saving the president's life.

General Bill Dryden stepped up to Dr. Newberry and saluted him crisply and addressed the team. "On behalf of a grateful nation and the president of the United States of America, I would like to personally thank you and the others for your bravery under extremely difficult circumstances. I have recommended to the president that you and those with you be given a special award for your heroism."

Chase was humbled by the general's recommendation and felt a tinge of guilt for not being who he said he was. "Thank you for your kind words. I am truly humbled by them. I am thankful for the opportunity to serve my president and the men and women who serve with him. I am only saddened that I—we could not have saved them all. Unfortunately, we had to leave our dead on the field of battle for the angry mob to desecrate," he said as tears welled up in his eyes and ran down his dusty cheek.

"Well, Doctor, we have plans for that bunch, and there will be a payback. On that you can rely." His eyes narrowed and a look of steel defined his face as he spoke. "Now," he said warmly, "is there anything I can get for you and your medical team?"

Chase looked down at the blood-soaked clothes he was wearing. "How about a change of clothes? I seem to be wearing the president's blood as well as several others."

"Yes, sir!" the general said enthusiastically. "I'll tell you what, I'll get you set up in one of our Guest Housing Units, and you can shower and change. Why don't you then get a good meal and a good night's sleep, and maybe we can squeeze in a tour of this old city before you guys ship out. There's a lot to see."

Chase looked at the others and smiled, "That sounds like a great idea. I think I'll take you up on that. Miss Hodges, how does that sound to you?"

Chase turned and looked at his assistant.

"Yes, sir! I could use a shower and a good night's sleep, as well," she said as she nervously looked around.

The general smiled genuinely. "Okay then, Dr. Newberry. If you will follow Lieutenant Anderson, he will get you squared away." Again he saluted Chase, turned on his heels, and retraced his steps.

Chapter 14

The City of Ramstein…

A strapping, young lieutenant stepped up, saluted, and said, "Sir, ma'am, if you will follow me, I'll get you squared away."

He guided them to a waiting jeep and took them to guest housing. He handed each of them a set of door keys after unlocking their doors.

"Sir, ma'am, I hope these accommodations will meet your needs. These are the best we have," he said as he scanned the suite. "Even three- and four-star generals and their families stay here when they pass through."

Chase took a cursory look around the suite. "Son, this is more than I expected, please express my thanks to the good general."

"Well then, if there is nothing more, here are the keys to the jeep, and I will see you at breakfast. I'll see to it that room service sends up a hearty meal to each of your rooms since we've already missed dinner. Oh, and by the way, there is a complete change of clothes for both of you in your closets."

The lieutenant gave them directions to the officer's mess hall and then left.

Chase quickly showered and hit the sack. Within a minute, he was asleep.

The next day was bright and sunny. Rays of the morning light shone through the curtains and filled the room where Chase slept. He woke up refreshed and hungry. It was the first good night's sleep he had gotten in the last forty-eight hours, and he didn't know when the next one would be. After making a few minor adjustments to his facial and body wear, he looked into the mirror to make sure everything was in place. The man in the mirror stared back at him with weary eyes. He hoped no one would notice.

He and Nurse Hodges had decided to meet for breakfast in the officer's dining room around ten a.m. Chase stepped out of his apartment wearing sandals, navy blue slacks, and a Hawaiian shirt. Nurse Hodges was already waiting for him in the jeep. She had on a pair of khaki capris and a white, loose-fitting blouse. She had a large sun hat on that covered most of her head, sunglasses, and a satchel-sized handbag.

"Good morning, Chase. Sleep well?" Nurse Hodges said with a smile in her voice.

He nodded. "Like a baby. I slept for a while, woke up, ate something, and went back to sleep," he said with a goofy grin. Then he started the engine and drove to the Officer's Dining Room for breakfast. As they finished, Lieutenant Anderson strode up to their table.

"Sir, ma'am, I trust you found everything in order and enjoyed your breakfast. For the rest of the day, I am at your service to take you on a sightseeing tour of Ramstein. I will take you wherever you would like to go. I know all of the major and minor points of interest."

Chase rubbed his hands together and looked at his nurse then back to the lieutenant. "Thank you. I've heard that the Ramstein Stadium is a great place to go to see a soccer—or football—game, as they call it. Is there a game today?"

A glint of understanding passed between the two men before a word was spoken. "Yes, as a matter of fact, there is a game this morning. When will you be ready to go?" Lieutenant Anderson asked.

Chase looked at Nurse Hodges, and they both stood to leave. Earlier that morning, Chase's handlers gave him additional instructions to follow, and this was where they started.

"We're ready now, let's go," then he paused as he remembered that he had left his medical kit back in the room.

"Oh, hold it just a minute, let me go back to my room and pick up my medical bag. You know what they say, 'Don't leave home without it,'" he explained with a wry smile.

"I've got to get my medical kit, as well," said Nurse Hodges, "so I'll be back in a minute, too."

The lieutenant nodded. "Okay then, let's meet back at the front of the officer's mess in five." With that, the three of them parted and reassembled right on time at the side of a waiting Humvee.

"Wow! This is riding in style!" Chase exclaimed.

"The ride isn't the best, but it's much safer than that jeep," Lieutenant Anderson said as he revved up the engine.

Chase took his seat in the front and wondered how they were going to ditch the lieutenant and not raise a lot of questions. At just about that time, his earpiece awoke with the voice of Mr. Tattoo.

"Don't worry about the lieutenant. He's one of us. Just follow the instructions I gave you earlier."

Chase nodded his head slightly.

What choice do I have? Chase thought. Chase picked up the end of the stethoscope, breathed on it as if he was polishing it, and smiled; they got the point.

The Humvee left the safety of Ramstein Air Force Base and headed to the Hauptverkehrsstrade, the inner ring of the sprawling city of Ramstein. They turned left on Landstuhler Street that led them to the stadium area. Traffic was light for that time of the day, and they were able to get to their destination without any problems.

As they approached the drop-off area in front of the stadium, the lieutenant turned to Dr. Newberry. "Sir, I'm going to drop you off at the ticketing area and wait for you in the vehicle. We don't like leaving government vehicles unattended in the city. When you have seen enough, just come out of the stadium, and I'll be watching for you and pick you up."

Chase thanked the lieutenant and exited the Humvee with Nurse Hodges close behind. "Okay, Miss Hodges, am I to assume that you are an FBI agent, too?" Chase asked as the two of them walked to the ticket booth.

Nurse Hodges hesitated a moment before answering his pointed question. It was obvious by the quizzed look on her face that she hadn't expected the question. "Let's just say that I'm on the side of the good guys, and you can call me Rachel when we are in private," she said with a whimsical tone in her voice.

"All right, Rachel. Where do we go from here?"

"Let's find our seats, and our contact will find us and lead us to the next connection. At this time we are functioning on a need-to-know basis," she said quietly.

"Rachel, are you wearing one of those earpieces, too?"

She pulled her hair back, revealing a similar device and then smiled.

"Do you hear what I am hearing in that thing?" Chase asked with a look of surprise on his face.

She nodded and winked.

They retrieved their tickets and proceeded into the stadium and found their seats. It was a warm day, and Chase ordered some soft drinks and popcorn, hoping that he could see at least the first half of the game before resuming his duties. But that was not to be.

Chapter 15

Air Force One, 30,000 feet over the Atlantic

A gentle hand touched the president's shoulder.

"Mr. President, Mr. President." He roused and spoke. "Yes?"

"Sir, you have been asleep for most of the flight but it is six a.m., Monday morning and I need to check your vitals. Would you mind sitting up for just a few minutes?" The new medical team assigned to the president had been monitoring his condition but needed to check his wound and change the bandages.

As the doctor gingerly lifted the wrapping from around the wound, he couldn't help but comment, "The doctor who saved your life did a great job. That piece of shrapnel nearly punctured your spleen. Removing it without an x-ray or MRI was like threading a needle blindfolded. This guy was either highly skilled in trauma surgery or very lucky," he said with a look of amazement in his hazel eyes.

The president squinted as the bright light of the sun flowed through the port-hole into the room. "I read his dossier, and he seemed to be very competent," the president replied.

An expression of concern crossed the doctor's face as he listened to the president's breathing. "As I examined you, I did notice that you had a place where the doctor drew blood. Do you remember anything about that?"

The president reflected for a moment then shook his head. "No, doc," he said as he scratched his chin thoughtfully. "I was in and out most of the time. The doctor attending me had a nurse at his side, but that's all I remember. Like I said, I was losing a lot of blood. Maybe that's where they gave me something for pain or an antibiotic."

In a veiled attempt to mask his concern, the doctor shrugged his shoulders. "Well, don't worry about it. You were in the best of hands, and I believe you will make a full recovery. Now get some more rest, and I'll see you in an hour or so."

The doctor stepped out of the medical clinic and walked down the corridor of Air Force One. He speed dialed someone high in the administration.

"Sir, we have a problem!" he said without emotion.

Washington, DC

In an apartment located in a run-down section of Washington, DC, another phone rang.

"Hello?" the Dean answered.

"Have you been able to get anything new from your guest?"

A moment of silence filled the airwaves.

"No, nothing new. I can assure you that we have tried everything short of water boarding."

"You know how vital it is that we get in contact with Mr. Newton, don't you?" asked the voice on the other end of the connection.

The Dean bristled at being questioned by an underling even though he was high in the administration. "Yes, yes, I don't need to be lectured by a governmental employee. I will keep the pressure on her. Hopefully within the next twenty-four hours, she will break. By then we should know something."

"Oh, by the way," said the caller cautiously, "You might be interested in knowing that Doctor Newberry drew blood from the president while he was unconscious."

The Dean's eyes narrowed, and he hesitated before answering. He spoke slowly so as to let his words sink in. "Now what would Doctor Newberry be doing drawing blood from the president?"

The caller considered his words carefully so as to not sound inept. "Sir, the best we can guess is to have it analyzed—possibly for its DNA," he said uncertainly.

The Dean's jaw tightened. "Thank you for that tidbit of information. I will increase the pressure on Mrs. Newton. I want you to find and eliminate Doctor Newberry. Leave no stone unturned. Do you understand?" he seethed.

"Oh, yes. Absolutely, sir," said the caller as the line went dead.

The Dean reentered the small dark cell where Megan sat, "Please try again, Mrs. Newton. It is urgent that we get in contact with your husband, and time is running out," the Dean said as he nodded to his assistant.

It was time for a new method of interrogation.

Chapter 16

Ramstein Stadium

The stadium was nearly filled, and the game was about to start when a man approached Chase.

"Doctor," said a man dressed as a soccer coach, "there is a man with a medical need. Would you mind coming with me and attending to his needs?"

Chase gave Nurse Hodges a questioning look and rose to his feet. Nurse Hodges stood, and the two excused themselves and slipped out of the stadium. Without speaking, the man led them out into the main passageway, which encircled the stadium. Then he took an exit that brought them out into the parking deck. Neither spoke, knowing that the man leading them was only following the instructions given to him.

Their guide pointed to a black Volvo taxicab parked along the curb, and in his best English said, "Please step into the car and go with them. Ask no questions. God's speed!" Then he turned and disappeared into the crowd of passersby.

Rachel looked at Chase curiously. "That was a comforting thing to say."

"It certainly was. We not only need God's speed but also His guidance and protection," replied Chase as he opened the door for Rachel and got in behind her. Chase's thoughts were a thousand miles away as he sat and looked out the passenger window at the changing scenery.

As they came to a stop at a halt sign, a black sedan with its windows darkened pulled alongside them. One of the windows rolled down, and a gun extended from the open window. The blast shattered the window of the vehicle Chase and Rachel were in, but no one was injured. The driver of Chase's car slammed the car into reverse, sped backward, and made a 180-degree turn and accelerated, leaving the attacker in the distance. A high-speed chase ensued. Shots were fired from the pursuers, most of the time missing their mark.

"Look!" exclaimed Chase as he peered out the back window. "A Humvee put itself between us and those guys who were shooting."

Rachel raised her head just enough to look over the back seat. "Yes, and they are returning fire at the guys in the car," she said breathlessly.

"Whoever it is is a pretty good shot. The driver in the pursuing car just got hit." Suddenly it swerved and struck a telephone pole. It flipped on its side and skidded sending sparks in every direction. Chase watched in horror as it rolled over and burst into flames.

The Humvee slowed and came to a halt as the car Chase and Rachel were in resumed its journey. The driver seemed unperturbed by the diversion. Twenty minutes later, the cab came to a stop in front of a ram-shackled building.

"Here we are," the cab driver announced. "This is the address I was instructed to take you. Please exit the car and go to that door," he said, indicating an unpretentious entry.

"I don't know how you do it, Doc, but you have a way of attracting attention wherever you go. We think they are on to our little plan and are out to get you," said the voice in Chase's ear. Chase picked up the stethoscope and gave it a questioning look. Then he turned to Rachel for guidance. She nodded for him to comply, and they exited the vehicle.

Shaken but unharmed, they cautiously walked up to the front door and knocked. To their surprise, they heard a metallic snap, and it eased open. They entered and followed the narrow corridor. After going through several more doors and hallways, they arrived at their destination, which was a fully operational medical lab.

A tall gentleman in a dark suit stepped up to them, smiled, and stuck his hand out.

"Welcome to the sovereign nation of the United States of America, Dr. Newberry and Miss Hodges." His voice sounded more like that of John Wayne than an FBI operative.

"I am Robert Gray, the department head of this FBI unit here in Ramstein. I understand your journey here was interesting."

The expression on their faces was priceless as Chase gave him a brief summation of their ride.

Agent Gray nodded knowingly. "Yes, we were aware of your little diversion and even anticipated it. We knew someone was monitoring our movements. We just don't know who or why."

Then he turned and looked at Nurse Hodges. "I believe you have something of value for me."

The two exchanged glances, and Nurse Hodges pulled a small vial of blood from her medical kit. "Is this what you are referring to?" she asked with an impish smile. Agent Gray eyed the flask of blood eagerly. "Yes, yes, it is. I would like to give this to the lab boys and let them have a shot at analyzing it. Once we get the DNA broken down, we can feed the information to our friends back in the States."

Rachel handed the small tube to Mr. Gray's extended hand and closed his fingers around it. "You two have done a great service for your country, and on behalf of Vice President James F. Randall, code word 'cakewalk,' we would like to thank you for you service to your country."

Gray's last statement jolted Chase back to reality. "According to your last statement, you obviously know what we are dealing with."

A look of steel crossed Gray's rugged face. "Yes, sir, I do and am deeply concerned. From our vantage point, there isn't much we in the military can do to remedy the situation in Washington, DC, but we certainly are glad to help you with your mission. Now is there anything I can get you?"

Chase stuck his hands onto his pockets and thought for a moment. He was clearly uncomfortable with all this attention. "No, sir, I don't believe we need anything," he said as he gave Rachel a sideways glance."

She shrugged her shoulders, indicating she agreed.

"Would you like to wait for the results?" Agent Gray continued.

"No, sir," Chase said as he pulled his hands from his pockets and looked at his watch. "I think that we had better be getting back to the stadium. I think our work is done here, and maybe we have time to catch the rest of the soccer game."

Agent Gray smiled knowingly. "Very well, then. I want to wish you God's speed on your return to the states." He saluted both Chase and Nurse Hodges, and Chase snapped to attention and returned the gesture.

Agent Gray turned to a desk, lifted an envelope and a box, and handed them to Chase. On the outside of the envelope were the instructions, "Do not open until you are airborne."

"I've been instructed to give you these before you leave. I trust that you will find everything in order," he said as the lieutenant approached.

The driver of the Humvee led them back to his vehicle. As they climbed back into the Hummer, the driver looked at Chase with an apologetic look. "I'm sorry to inform you, but the game ended a few minutes ago. We need to be returning to the base."

Chase tugged on his ear thoughtfully as he considered asking for a short tour of the city. He vetoed the idea before pressing the issue. Their ride back to the base was quiet and uneventful. Rachel let out a sigh of relief as they came within sight of the sprawling military base.

The guards at the main gate saluted and signaled the driver to proceed without being stopped and searched. Rather than going back to the base commander's office, the driver delivered them to his personal residence. General Dryden stepped out of his front door and greeted Chase and Rachel as they exited the hummer. "Well, doctor, I trust you had an enjoyable time in our fair city." He paused but not long enough for Chase to respond. Then his tone changed, "However, it looks like your stay will be cut a little short. We have a plane waiting for you as we speak, and they would like very much if you would board so they can get underway. You might be interested in knowing that plane is loaded with soldiers leaving the Afghanistan war zone and are anxious to get home for a long-awaited leave."

Chase followed the general's gaze as he looked in the direction of the airfield. Then he turned back and nodded.

"Of course, General, we would be more than happy to accompany them. Where do we go?" asked Chase as he squinted in the distance.

The general gave his subordinate a quick nod.

"The lieutenant will see to it that you get to the right plane. I wouldn't want you to fly off in the wrong direction," he said with a whimsical smile. "Again, let me say how grateful we all are for your heroic effort on behalf of our nation." Rather than saluting Chase, he stuck out his hand and gripped Chase's firmly.

They reloaded the hummer, and the lieutenant drove them to the far end of the base where the departing planes sat waiting for clearance. He guided Chase and Rachel to the jumbo jet. They climbed the stairs and entered the mammoth plane. At first glance Chase noticed that the plane was nearly filled with men and women in BDU's. A look of anxiety and weariness filled their eyes as they observed the two civilians entering their plane. The young lieutenant guided Chase and Rachel to their seats in the first-class seating. Only after they were seated and buckled in could they begin to relax.

Within twenty minutes the giant plane was lumbering down the runway and lifted off. "This is a far cry better than the last time we caught a ride on a plane," Rachel said as she kicked off her sandals.

Chase shook his head. "I don't know. I kind of liked the way we got onto that last plane," he said with a mischievous look in his eyes.

Once they were airborne, Chase took out the envelope and carefully opened it. Inside were two new IDs, passports, and money. Instructions were also typed out for each of them to follow. At the bottom of the list of instructions was a hand-written note to Chase. It was written from Mr. Tattoo.

"I don't want you to worry. We are doing everything in our power, but your wife has been abducted," the note read.

"Abducted! My wife has been abducted?" Chase cried. "How could that be?" he said out loud.

The outburst jolted dozens of battle-weary, homesick solders to the reality that no one was safe—even in America. The news shocked them like an incoming round.

"I thought that the FBI sent an agent by to be her personal bodyguard," said Rachel with a look of concern on her face.

"Quiet, you idiot! You want to get the whole plane load of soldiers up in arms?" said the unknown voice in his earpiece.

Just then Chase looked around him and saw every eye in the plane staring at him. He gulped and smiled sheepishly and sat back in his seat.

"Somebody has abducted my wife, and you didn't tell me?" Chase said as he looked at his stethoscope.

The voice came back. "Sorry, we couldn't tell you for fear of compromising the mission, but let me assure you that we are doing everything in our power to locate your wife," said the voice tenderly.

Rachel gently placed her hand on Chase's arm. "Oh, Chase, I am so sorry," Nurse Hodges said.

Chase's head jerked up as if pulled by a rope. "You just called me Chase. No one but a very few people even know who I am, and you just blurted out my real name for the whole plane to hear. Who are you, anyway?" His eyes narrowed as he looked down at her.

Suddenly it clicked. "You're not Rachel or Nurse Hodges. You are Jennifer Tibbits, aren't you?"

She hesitated a moment then slowly nodded her head. A light smile parted her lips. "I wouldn't have recognized you had I not been told in advance."

A wave of mixed emotions swept over Chase, dormant feelings long denied, long suppressed, germinated in the soil of his heart and pressed their way upward. He was glad to have Jennifer at his side again, but then a tinge of guilt pricked his heart. And his thoughts turned to his wife.

"They got M, Jennifer. They got my wife."

"I know. I'm so sorry, Chase," she said with pain in her voice.

There was an uncomfortable pause in the conversation. Then Chase looked over at Jennifer. "It never even dawned on me that it was you. I didn't recognize you at all."

Jennifer brushed a few strands of hair behind her ear.

"Yeah, those guys back at the tattoo shop can work miracles," she said as she looked at herself in the reflection of a window.

Chase scratched his neck. "Do you mean that they sent you to the same dingy tattoo shop as they sent me? What do you think of Mr. Ta—"

The look on Jennifer's face reminded him that their every word was being monitored back at the tattoo shop.

A moment later Chase's phone vibrated. He looked at the caller ID. Megan!

Chapter 17

Washington, D.C...

The sight of the Washington, DC, skyline was a bit intimidating as Sheriff Conyers entered the first mix-master. He was used to the wide open spaces of Colorado and the traffic, the smog, and the crush of people were more than he expected.

After driving nearly non-stop from Beaumont to Washington, DC, he was road weary, but ready for action. The only problem was that in a city this big, he had no idea where to begin.

His deputy had called him earlier in the day and told him that a strange vehicle had been roaming the streets. It was obvious that someone was looking for him, and he was glad he left when he did. But now he had to focus on his mission. To his thinking, the best place to begin was to start by circling the *New York Times* building, hoping to catch a glimpse of someone he knew. So he nosed his cruiser in the direction of the downtown area. Unfortunately for him, it was rush-hour, and since he didn't know the area, he got turned around and ended up on a one-way street going the wrong way. It wasn't long before the Sheriff was lost. So he drove over to a tree-lined park and stopped along the curb and prayed. His was a simple prayer from a heart of simple faith.

"Lord, I'm not as lost as I once was, but I'm as lost as a man can get in this big place. Would you lead me to where I can do the most good? In Jesus's name, amen."

While he waited, he fell asleep. How long he slept, he didn't know. It was at least the rest of that day and all though the night. On Saturday morning Sheriff Conyers woke up hungry and with a sense of mission. He pulled out into traffic and looked for the first diner with a crowd of police cars and firefighters. He found just what he was looking for and went in.

He took a seat at the counter and ordered his favorite—steak and eggs.

The officer next to him cocked his head mid-bite. "I take it you're not from around here."

Conyers smirked and looked at his uniform, "How could you tell?"

The burly police officer next to him craned his neck. "Your service cruiser, your uniform, and heck, even your gun. Now I'd like to see some identification if you don't mind." The officer stood and reached back and released his sidearm.

The sheriff held up his hands. "Alright, friend. I'm one of you. Just let me pull out my wallet from my back pocket."

Slowly he reached behind him and gingerly lifted his wallet out and showed him his identification. Satisfied, the policeman sat down, but by then he had a number of other officer's attention. "You can't be too careful anymore. Now what brings you to our fair city?"

Sensing this was one of those serendipitous divine encounters, the sheriff decided to enlist the help of his fellow officers. "I am looking for a friend of mine, a reporter, a man named, Chase Newton."

To many of them, it was a household name.

"Chase Newton with the *New York Times*? Yeah, I know him, or at least I read his articles. He's good!" said the officer as he resumed his breakfast.

"You do know the *New York Times* was bombed the other day, don't you?" he continued.

Conyers took a sip of his coffee and looked over at his acquaintance. He voice saddened. "Yeah, I read about it, I knew the editor too. He is, or was from my hometown, Beaumont. Mr. Newton's life is in grave danger and I need to find him fast.

He got a call right after the assassinations from a man claiming to be James F. Randall. We are convinced that the man in the White House is an imposter. Mr. Berkowitz was killed because he and Chase Newton are working together to expose him. The ones who killed Stan are looking for Chase and will kill him on sight."

Conyers leaned forward and put his elbows on the counter. "Look, guys, can I count on your help?"

The captain of the local precinct, a man with sandy-colored hair and a young face, spoke up as he reached into his pocket and produced a small card with his cell number written on it. "Look, Sheriff, just call me, and I'll get the word out in a hurry."

"I can't thank you enough, Captain. That means a lot to me." Then the two men shook hands.

The US Naval Observatory

As a result of the assassination and attempt on his life, Vice President Randall went into hiding in a nearby hotel. He knew he couldn't stay there long, so he came up with a plan. He exchanged his street clothes for his personal bodyguard's and slipped back into his personal residence on Observation Circle under the cover of darkness.

With his security detail beefed up, he felt he was relatively safe. Plus, everyone on the compound was sequestered, and absolutely no one was to communicate with the outside, and no one was to leave the property. Everyone was more than glad to comply, knowing that the fate of the country hung in the balance. His home became a fortress under siege. The head of his security detail unlocked the small arsenal of weapons stashed in the basement and distributed them to all the staff from the secretaries down to the cooks. Then he gave them a crash course on how to use the weapons. He just hoped that the incoming vice president wouldn't need the residence for a few more weeks.

While preparations were being made for his protection, the vice president picked up his phone and tried Chase's cell phone again. It rang several times before Chase answered it.

Chapter 18

Washington, D.C...

"Hello, Megan?" Chase said tentatively.

"Chase, I'm—" The phone was ripped from her trembling hand.

"Mr. Newton," said the Dean as he interrupted Megan midsentence. "It is so good to talk with you. I believe we have a guest with us who would love very much to speak with you, but first we have a little business to transact." He eyed Megan lustfully as he spoke.

"By the way, I have not had the honor of meeting you personally, but you may remember one of my protégées, Pastor T.J. Richards?"

At the mention of that name, Chase's mind was awash with angry emotions. Then he remembered a verse of scripture he had committed to memory. "Vengeance is mine, the Lord says, I will repay." The verse brought him a spirit of calm, but still he feared what awaited him and Megan.

His jaw tightened. "Who are you, and what do you want with me?" he finally asked through clinched teeth.

"Oh, yes, my name is unimportant," he said with the wave of his hand, "but for the record, they call me 'Dean,' or 'the Dean' because I spent so many years in the education business training young, impressionable minds to think on a higher plane. But I digress. I still have not gotten over the way you spoke to T.J. at your last meeting. I plan to rectify that when we meet," he said with a sneer in his voice.

Chase lost no time in making his demands known. "What are you doing with my wife? Why have you taken her? She's done nothing and knows nothing. Let her go!" Chase demanded while Jennifer sat wide-eyed.

"All in good time, all in good time, but first I have a proposition for you." The Dean calmly replied. He paused to let the tension build. "You tell me where your Mr. Randall is and your wife will live to see another day. If not, her life will end suddenly and violently. Do you understand?" The Dean paced back and forth as he spoke.

Chase clutched the arm of his chair as he tried desperately to control his emotions. "I don't know where the vice president is. I have only spoken with him a few times since the assassination attempt," he said as he desperately tried to assess the situation.

"Then you had better find out where he is or," he paused for effect, "or your wife dies," the Dean let his voice trail off.

Chase was frantic, angry, and at a total loss for words. Jennifer tried to console him, but he was at his wits' end. He needed a miracle and fast.

The Dean continued his verbal onslaught. "I understand that you impersonated a doctor and you or your nurse took something from the president. I wonder if you could tell me what it was." Chase's mind raced; he tried to bluff.

"What are you talking about? I saved the president's life, for crying out loud."

Suddenly the phone reverberated with the sound of gun fire.

Chase's heart pounded in his chest. "What was that?" He was frantic. All he could think of was his wife lying dead.

"Oh, so sorry," the Dean said nonchalantly. "My gun has a hair trigger and accidentally discharged, but I think it missed her. Let's see, yes, she is still breathing. Now you were saying?" He paused. "Yes, you were about to tell me what you took from the president and for what purpose."

Defeated at the game of cat and mouse, Chase admitted that he had taken a sample of the president's blood in order to get a DNA analysis.

"What will that prove, you fool? When the old Mr. Randall is dead and gone, there will be nothing to compare it to. It will make no difference, and all of your pathetic efforts will be in vain," he said in a triumphant tone. "Now it is Monday, seven a.m. Eastern Standard Time, so find the vice president within the next forty-eight hours, or your wife dies," and hung up.

The look on Jennifer's face said it all.

"Did you guys get all that?" Chase asked. "We have big problems, and I need your help big time."

"Yes, Chase, we heard," said Mr. Tattoo, "and we're on it. We have our best people working all their sources. It won't be long before we get a lead on her. By the way, the police found our operative a few days ago in her car with a shot to the head. Someone must have slipped a bug inside Stan's office before he discovered the one in his lampshade."

Chase closed his eyes and thought back a week ago.

"There was a man coming out of Stan's office the day I broke the news to him. His name is Senator Max Wilcox. He had to have planted the bug."

"Then these guys were on to us from the get go," his contact back in Washington said as he tilted his chair back on two legs.

"But they don't know where the vice president is—at least not yet," Chase reiterated as he rubbed his forehead. By now a tension headache was bearing down on him, like a locomotive.

Mr. Tattoo sighed heavily. "Yeah, but they got your wife, and they want you to lead them right to him. Oh, and by the way, they will probably kill you and your wife as an extra bonus."

"I know, I know," said Chase wearily. "I've already taken that into consideration. If we get into a worst case scenario, we are ready to meet the Lord, but I just hate the idea of jeopardizing the life of the vice president or anyone else."

Just then Chase's cell phone vibrated.

"Look, I have to take this call." Chase held his phone in front of him and pushed the call button. "Hello, Mr. Vice President."

The voice on the other end of the line said, "Code word 'cakewalk.'"

Chase answered succinctly, "Crosswalk."

"Is this a good time to talk?" the vice president asked.

Chase looked around the cabin of the giant plane with a tense smile.

"Yes, Mr. Vice President, it is a very good time to talk. I'm on a plane from Ramstein Air Force Base loaded with soldiers coming out of Iraq and Afghanistan." Keeping his voice to a whisper, he said, "But sir, I, or rather, we have a huge problem."

"Oh? What's new? Tell me about it, son."

"Well, first of all, I just got a call from a man calling himself the Dean, and he informed me that he and his henchmen have abducted my wife. They are demanding that I lead them to wherever you are. Next, I just found out that Stan's office was bugged the day that I went in and broke the story to him. They know about Dr. Cleve Newberry and his nurse taking a sample of the president's blood to have a DNA analysis done on it. They have given me forty-eight hours to turn you over to them, or my wife dies." Chase's voice sounded strange, unreal even to himself as he spoke. The drone of the jet's engines drowned out the uncomfortable pause.

"Well, we can't let that happen, now, can we? Look, I have some documentation to prove that laws were broken and that foreign influences and agents have infiltrated our government. Some of those people who sit in very high places are not even citizens of the United States. We will have to be very careful, however, with whom we talk. I know of several people who can help us, but we must act fast." His voice carried a tone of determination. Chase was encouraged.

If this man ever makes it to the presidency, he will make a good one, he thought.

The stress he was feeling caused his neck to spasm. He tried to loosen it up by stretching, but with the phone pressed tightly against his ear, his movements were limited. He pulled the phone from his ear long enough to put it on speaker so that Jennifer could listen in to the conversation between him and the vice president. She was clearly interested in finding Megan and saving the life of the man she heard speaking on the phone.

"You said, 'Documentation,' and that reminded me of something. Before Glenn died, he told me to check his laptop because he had a lot of information on it that could be used to uncover this plot."

The vice president's voice took on a renewed interest. "Where is the laptop now?"

Chase didn't miss a beat. "It's in the SUV I rented and left back in DC." The vice president nodded in acknowledgment. "Can you get to it?"

Chase's mind pictured the SUV sitting where he left it with a bomb strapped to its underbelly. "It's too risky, even disguised as Dr. Newberry. They probably followed my paper trail and are watching the car around the clock. Either that or they have placed a bomb under it. The good thing is that I don't think they know about the laptop. I just hope they haven't found it," said Chase as clouds whisked past his window.

He looked around to see if anyone was listening, but to his relief they were either sleeping or watching the on-board movie.

Jennifer leaned in close to the phone. "Mr. Vice President, this is Rachel Hodges, Dr. Newberry's nurse assistant. We need to get a DNA sample from you so the guys in the lab can do an analysis and comparison. How do you propose we do that?"

There was a slight pause as Vice President Randall thought about his options. He spoke with determination.

"Despite the risks, we are going to have to meet somewhere. I'll give you a blood sample and whatever information I have then. With what you have on Glenn's laptop, you should have the upper hand on this bunch."

Jennifer leaned back and let Chase take the lead again. "We know who they are. They call themselves the Order. We have had dealings with them over four years ago with that Document thing. Do you remember?"

The vice president's face clouded, and his voice took on an ominous tone. "Oh yes, I remember. I was not involved, but I followed the events closely. Back then I was just a junior senator of the minority party and was barely noticed by the guys running the White House or the Congress, for that matter. After you broke the story, I was on one of the committees investigating that bunch. I, too, am quite aware of the Order."

"Then you know they cannot to be taken lightly. They have killed once and will do it again when they feel threatened," said Chase with weariness in his voice. "And right now you and I are a big threat to them." He stared out of the window.

The vice president leaned back in his chair. His face clouded. "Up until a week ago, I received daily briefs on the movements of the Order, but now I am beginning to think the information they gave me was flawed."

"Knowing what I now know, you're probably right," Chase answered as he rubbed the back of his neck. By now, the migraine was beginning to affect his thinking.

"What time will you to land?" inquired the vice president, as a plan began to formulate in his mind.

Jennifer could see that Chase needed some relief. She brushed her hair back and leaned into the phone.

"We should be landing at Dulles within the hour. Look, we know they will be looking for us, so we are going to have to change identities before we deplane, or they will capture us right off the bat. After we get out of the airport, we'll rent a car using our new identities. After that, we'll have to plan our next move."

Chase leaned back in his seat and closed his eyes, hoping for some relief from the pain he was feeling when another call beeped in. "Look, Mr. Vice President, I've got an incoming call, and it might be Megan. I need to take it."

"Okay, I'll get off the phone. Again, let me say thank you for all that you have done and will do."

As Chase fielded the incoming call, Jennifer excused herself and went to the restroom. She returned with a couple of bottles of water she had gotten from one of the flight attendants. She found some extra strength aspirin and handed them to Chase. He smiled back at Jennifer, popped the pills in his mouth, and washed them down with a big swig. "Thanks, I needed that," he said ruefully.

Despite the risk to the aircraft's flight data, Chase needed to take these calls. He rightly assumed the consequences of not taking them out weighed the danger to the plane or a fine from the FAA, so he took the call.

"Hello?" Sheriff Conyers let out a sigh of relief. "Chase, is that you?"

Chase's eyes widened. "Yes it's me, what's going on?"

"I just thought I'd try your cell one more time. Man, I've been driving around this city for what seems like days looking for you. Where are you?" the sheriff said with a tinge of frustration.

Chase glanced over at Jennifer and gave her a confused look. "Sheriff, what city are you talking about? You're not talking about Beaumont, are you?"

"No! I'm in Washington, DC," he exclaimed.

Chase straightened.

"Washington DC!" he repeated. "How'd you get there?"

Without hesitation, Sheriff Conyers said, "I drove here like you did, Chase. Now I've been looking all over for you. Where are you?" he said as he swerved around a corner and found an empty parking spot. He brought the police cruiser to an abrupt halt and listened.

Chase was incredulous. "I'm in a plane, and I'm about an hour out from Dulles International Airport."

"A plane!" His face etched in surprise. "Why are you on an airplane?"

"Look," said Chase, "I'll fill you in on all that when I see you. Right now my phone battery is running low. Could you wait for us in the arrival pick-up area?"

The sheriff pushed the brim of his hat back and he rubbed his forehead. "Yeah, sure," he said with a congenial tone.

"Now I need to warn you, I don't look like myself." Chase observed as he took a quick peek at Jennifer.

"Oh! Is that right? Who will you look like?" said Conyers as a question formed on his stubbly face.

"When you get here, look for two people dressed as tourists with colorful hats and sunglasses. Oh, and by the way, they are a mixed couple," he said as he gave Jennifer a mischievous look.

The total effect of his statement was striking. "A mixed couple. What do you mean by that?" Conyers pressed.

"You know, a black man and a white lady—that kind of mixed couple," Chase said with a smile in his voice.

"Oh, that kind. I get it. Who are you with, anyway?" Conyers inquired.

Not wanting to say too much or blow her cover, Chase opted to keep the good Sheriff guessing. "Let's just say she's a very good friend of yours," he said cryptically.

His eyebrows arched. "I can't wait to meet her. I'll be waiting for you two in my police cruiser," the sheriff said as he ended the conversation.

Chapter 19

Dulles International Airport...

Using a new GPS, which he purchased from a local electronics shop, Sheriff Conyers had no difficulty in finding his way to Dulles International Airport. He pulled up to the curb marked No Parking and waited. When a police officer approached his car, he simply showed him his badge, and the officer saluted and left.

Earlier in the day, Chase and Jennifer opened the box and found a couple of Hawaiian shirts and large-brimmed hats. Underneath the hats was several hundred dollars in cash, new credit cards, and driver's licenses. Chase was amused as he inspected his new apparel.

"I guess the more attention you draw to yourself, the less likely you are to be seen," Jennifer said, as she held her new flower-covered blouse. They each took turns going to the airplane's rest room and changing clothes. By the time the plane arrived, Dr. Newberry and Nurse Hodges didn't exist any longer; instead, a lovely couple from Jamaica emerged from the plane, stepped out of the terminal, and looked around.

The sheriff, who wasn't paying particular attention to the Jamaican couple as they approached his car, jolted as the gentleman in a flowered shirt opened the door and allowed a lady wearing a large brimmed hat to step in.

"You did good, Sheriff," Chase said as he pulled the door shut.

The sheriff did a double-take. "Chase, is that you? I'd never have recognized you. A wide grin spread across Chase's dark skin. "That's the plan Sheriff," Chase said. "Do you think that anybody spotted us?"

Conyers glanced in his rearview mirror before answering. "I doubt it. You two just blended in like all the other people dressed weird," he said with a smile.

"Weird? I'll have you know that this shirt cost two bucks at Goodwill!" said the voice in Chase's earpiece.

"By the way, who is your friend?" the sheriff asked as he tried to get a better look at the woman in the colorful hat.

Jennifer acted nonplused. "Why, Sheriff, I'm crushed, after all this time you didn't recognize me?"

The police cruiser nearly swerved into the oncoming lane as the sheriff gawked on the mirror. "Miss Jennifer, I'd never have recognized you either. Why the disguises?"

Chase deliberated a moment trying to think of a succinct answer. "Look, Sheriff, it's a long story but suffice it to say, we are a part of an undercover operation and the same people who killed the president are looking us."

"I know. My deputy called me as I was driving here and informed me that a strange car was cruising the streets of Beaumont."

As they passed through yet another congested intersection, Sheriff Conyers gave a quick glance at

Chase. Do you have any idea where we are going? I sure could use a little guidance."

Chase leaned over the front seat. "Yes, we need to go someplace safe and do some quick planning. The vice president will be calling me within the hour, and I need to tell him what the next move is."

Conyers gave him a big grin. "I know of the perfect place. It's the diner where I had breakfast. We just might be able to get some reinforcements while we're there, too."

The sheriff nosed the car into the DC traffic and headed to the diner. With his new GPS giving him directions, he made the journey without once missing a turn. He turned into the parking lot and guided the police cruiser into an empty parking slot. He then reached over and patted his new toy on its top. "This is the first time to my knowledge that a woman had a better sense of direction than me," he said with a crooked smile.

Jennifer rolled her eyes and shook her head. "Oh brother, not you too."

The sheriff shrugged his shoulders innocently. "What'd I say?"

Chase patted him on the back. "Don't worry about it, Sheriff. I know what you meant." He winked.

Conyers smiled. "Look, guys, how about I go in and scope out the place first?"

Chase cut his eyes in Jennifer's direction. "That's a good idea. We'll sit tight until you tell us to come in."

He was gone only a minute and came back with the all-clear sign. Chase and Jennifer cautiously got out and made their way into the diner.

The lunch crowd had thinned out, leaving a few police officers finishing up on the house specialty, apple pie *al a mode*. To one side there were some county workers, but other than that, the trio had the place to themselves.

At Chase's behest they pushed their way farther into the small seating area.

"Let's sit in the back and face the entrance," Chase suggested.

A friendly waitress greeted them but took a special interest in the sheriff. She made sure that his coffee cup was never less than half empty, and she was more than willing to dominate the conversation if it involved talking to him. It was obvious to Chase and Jennifer that she was a very lonely woman. The thought never occurred to the good sheriff. Finally, to the relief of Chase and Jennifer, the waitress moved on to other patrons and left them alone. Over lunch, Chase filled the sheriff in on all that happened, and the sheriff listened and scribbled a few notes on a napkin.

Once they were all up to speed, Chase shifted gears. "Look, Sheriff, I must to get to the SUV I rented a few days ago, but I know it will be watched. How do you propose we do that?" Chase asked.

Conyers took a swig of coffee before answering. Then he looked at Chase with a whimsical smile. "That's simple, Chase. I'm a police officer responding to a report of a stolen vehicle, and I might add that according to the car rental office, it is stolen, and you are wanted for grand auto theft."

A look of surprise swept over Chase's weary face. "Great, now I can add that to the list of things I'm wanted for—stealing an SUV."

Stranger in the White House

Conyers gave Jennifer a wink and broke out in laughter at seeing his friend squirm a little. "That's okay. I think I can work things out with the rental company since it's your first offense. Now where's the car parked?" he asked with raised eyebrows.

Chase lifted his hand and rubbed the back of his neck nervously as he tried to remember where he left the car. "It's in a parking garage at Eleventh and Clifton Street. But be careful. There could be a car bomb, or someone could be sitting in a nearby car, waiting to shoot whoever comes near that car."

Conyers leaned his elbows on the table as the waitress approached with a fresh pot of coffee.

"Well, before I go and get my head blown off, I think I'll call in a favor." He reached into his uniform pocket and pulled out the card given to him by the young precinct captain and dialed the number.

"Hello, Captain, this is Sheriff Conyers. I have a favor to ask of you. Could you send a bomb squad to the parking garage at the end of Eleventh and Clifton Street? There's an SUV sitting there, and I have a hunch there just might be a bomb underneath it."

"If there's another bomb threat, I need to get my team on to it now. I'll send my bomb squad out there as soon as possible. Thanks for the heads up, Sheriff."

Conyers smiled. "Great, I'll meet you there." Then he closed his phone and gave a triumphant grin to his friend.

Chase's expression went blank for a moment. Then he shook his head in amazement.

"You sure get connected fast around here, don't you, Sheriff?" Jennifer said as she watched the waitress warily.

Conyers nodded and look up at the overly friendly waitress. "Well, it's not always what you know," Conyers said with a swelled chest, "but who you know in this city." Then he handed a generous tip to the waitress.

Chapter 20

Washington, DC...

When the bomb squad raced through the city streets, no one took much notice, as they blended into the everyday fabric of life in DC. When they arrived, they cordoned off the area so as to protect any bystanders. Yellow police tape greeted Sheriff Conyers as he neared the parking garage. He watched a team of skilled men maneuver into position a remote bomb-sniffing vehicle, which looked like a toy truck. He heard a cheer as they found what they were looking for.

"There it is," said the squad leader to Conyers. "It's a good thing you didn't go barging up to that SUV of yours. You would have been blown to smithereens. Give the guys a few minutes, and they'll have that thing disarmed, and we will take the vehicle to the police barn where we will go over it with a fine-tooth comb, looking for fingerprints." His voice was calm but pierced with a noticeable trace of tenseness.

Just as they were about to drive off with it, Sheriff Conyers made one request. "Look, Captain, I believe that there is some important evidence inside that SUV that I need for an ongoing investigation. Before you take off with it, could I check it out?"

The captain looked up from his paperwork. His eyes narrowed for a moment as he thought through the request.

"Yes, of course," he said decisively. "But wear a pair of rubber gloves. I don't want the evidence contaminated by any foreign fingerprints."

Conyers relaxed and gave him a big smile. "Sure thing, Captain," he said as he pulled on a pair of latex gloves.

Even though he knew it was safe, he still approached the SUV with caution. He opened the passenger side door and carefully removed the laptop, thanked the captain, and returned to the diner.

While Conyers was retrieving the laptop, Chase and Jennifer were catching up on each other's lives. Chase told her about his wedding. She listened intently. They filled the remaining time with small talk.

"I am so happy for you and Megan. I saw that coming a mile away. All the time you were working at the bank, I knew something was going on with you two. Whenever she was around, you acted like a junior high school boy." A distant look filled her eyes and she reflected on those days in Beaumont.

"Do you miss it?"

Jennifer cocked her head. "Miss what?"

"You know, the intrigue, the challenge of those days."

"No," she paused. "Those days are gone and I've moved on to bigger and better things."

"Anybody in your life?"

Her eyes refocused on Chase and made him nervous. "Nope, my life is too complex to allow anyone to get close. Always getting shipped off to solve some international crisis without explanation. I just couldn't do that to a boyfriend or husband."

Suddenly Chase felt the tug of guilt as he thought about Megan not knowing what was happening and he got homesick.

"I sure wish I could talk to M. It's been over a week and I miss her so much."

Jennifer reached over to squeeze his hand but stopped short and sighed. The moment was broken as Sheriff Conyers entered the diner to the delight of the waitress who seemed to have claimed him as her own. But rather than letting her distract him, he made a beeline to the table where Chase and Jennifer were sitting.

"You better be glad you didn't try to go somewhere in that SUV. You would have been blown to pieces. Here's the laptop," he said as he eyed the waitress. "How about we go down to the local police precinct and check it out? I'll feel much safer in that kind of environment."

Jennifer, who was growing increasingly anxious, was more than happy to get out of the diner. The two men quickly agreed.

Using his GPS, he was able to find his way to the nearest police precinct. The duty officer, the man who sat next to him at the diner, greeted the sheriff and directed him and the others to a private workspace where they could log on to the Internet. Within a few minutes, they were looking at the mother load of very damaging documents.

Conyers let out a low whistle as he stared at the screen. "This stuff implicates the president, Senator Max Wilcox, a sitting Supreme Court judge, a Secretary of the Treasury, the Justice of the Sixth District Court of

Appeals, and several senators." His forehead wrinkled under his police hat.

"Look here," Jennifer pointed to a sidebar, "there are links to the money source and off-shore banking accounts. It looks like this conspiracy goes up to the highest seats in our government."

Jennifer stood and started pacing the floor. "I knew Dad was working on something very important since he retired from the agency, but this is big—really big."

"Yeah, and it's probably what got him killed, too," the sheriff said, not realizing that Jennifer did not know her father was killed over a week ago back in Beaumont.

Suddenly a look of shock came over Jennifer. "Did you say that my dad is dead?" Tears welled up in her eyes, and she began to weep uncontrollably.

Realizing his oversight, Conyers wrapped his burly arms around Jennifer in a fatherly fashion and embraced her. "Oh, Jennifer, I'm so sorry. I didn't realize that no one had told you that your father was dead..." he let his voice trail off.

After an uncomfortable silence, he continued. "I had no idea that you didn't know." Then he gave Chase a questioning look as if to say, "Why haven't you told her?"

Through tearstained eyes, Jennifer looked at Chase and asked, "Did you know, too, Chase?"

Chase's gaze dropped to the floor as he had to admit his oversight. "Yes, I knew but couldn't tell you before now. It was just recently that I even found out who you were," he said in his defense.

"You knew and didn't tell me!"

Her words pierced his heart like a lance.

"I'm so sorry, Jennifer. I'm so sorry!" His voice was thick with emotion. He was grieving the loss of his friend.

Silence reigned for the next several minutes until Jennifer regained her composure. Finally she reached down and picked up her overstuffed purse and rooted around in it until she found a pack of tissues. She wiped her eyes and attempted to act normal, but Chase could tell she had erected a wall around her heart. It was there maybe to keep the pain in or keep people out—him out. He couldn't tell.

She spoke softly. "I knew that's the way Dad would go. He lived passionately for two things: his God and his country. I hope he finished well for both of them."

Finally Chase spoke. "If it's any consolation, I can say that he did." He paused a moment to clear his throat. "I was there when it happened. He gave his life serving the country he loved. And, Jennifer, I know that he had the peace of God that passes all understanding when he crossed over into God's presence," Chase added softly.

Jennifer seemed to soften a bit. "That's a comfort to know."

"How did it happen, anyway?" Jennifer finally asked after a few moments.

For the next few minutes, Chase related the events that led to her father's death then paused to give her time to reflect.

"Dad was such a great guy. He loved the hunt, the chase. It was like fishing to him, once he got the hook set, he just reeled them in. Retiring was one of the hardest things I ever saw him do." She paused and smiled through her tears. "Actually, between you and me, I don't think he ever really stopped working."

Chase and the sheriff sat staring at the computer until Conyers finally cleared his throat and wiped the tears from his eyes and looked at Jennifer. "I will admit we had a really great funeral service for your dad. He would have been embarrassed by all the kind words the people of the church and town said about him. He'll probably go down as a local hero or something. Heck, they just might put a statue in the center of the town square in his honor," he added to lighten the mood.

Chase, sensing the urgency of the hour and pain they all were feeling, stood, "Guys, let's pray right now," he said. "We need God's peace, protection, and providential guidance big time."

They prayed, and as their prayer time ended, Chase's cell phone vibrated again. It was the president.

Chapter 21

Naval Observatory

Vice President Randall was not a man to sit idly by and do nothing. He and his staff had been working for hours, planning his escape from his residence and planning how to get the incriminating evidence into the hands of the right people. Their options were rather thin. The evidence implicated many of the people he knew and trusted were involved in the conspiracy, and there were only a few people in the government who had not been compromised. Of them were the secretary of state, the secretary of defense, and the secretary of homeland security. How many of their subordinates could be trusted was not known. His notes did not say. He also knew that the justice of District Court of Appeals in Washington, DC, was not compromised and so a plan began to emerge, but how to implement it was the problem.

"Well, Carl, now that you have reviewed my plan, what do you think?" asked Vice President Randall, crossing his arms.

He looked up skeptically and answered without hesitation.

"Mr. Vice President, this plan is very risky and has several flaws in it," said the head of his security detail.

The vice president glanced up from the sheet of paper he was holding. "Oh? How so?" he inquired.

His friend Carl, the head of security, took a seat directly in front of him and scanned the face of the man he was sworn to protect. "Well, for starters, what if someone is watching the compound or the riverside? You would be a sitting duck."

Randall rubbed his weary eyes and considered his statement. "Okay, let's step back and rethink this whole plan. Then I'll call Chase."

After an hour of hashing it out, he dialed Chase's number; it was busy.

The phone call that Chase received was not from his wife, neither was it from the vice president.

"Hello!" Chase's face bore a look of expectancy as he answered the call. "Dr. Newberry, you've been a busy man," the president said in an overly friendly voice.

Again Chase sat in stunned silence, his mind reeling.

"Now before we get down to the real reason for my call, let me express my appreciation and the gratitude of this nation for your heroism. You not only saved my life but a number of your countrymen in the face of certain death, and I am personally grateful." The president paused as he segued to a more sober tone of voice.

"However, it's too bad that you will not enjoy the fruits of your labor." He paused and allowed time for Chase to follow his line of reasoning. "It seems while I was incapacitated, you performed a medical procedure, which I would not have approved of had I been of sound mind. You violated the law and your oath of office. It gives me great sadness to inform you that you won't be serving on my medical detail any longer." Again he paused to take a sip of water before he unleashed his next bombshell. "As a matter of fact, I need you to turn yourself over to the authorities without delay. If you do so immediately, I will personally go to bat for you and see to it that those nasty charges could be dropped. If not, you will be apprehended and tried for treason. You see, we know what you are up to, and we are prepared to go to whatever lengths we need to, to put a halt to this foolish and harebrained idea of yours." The president paused to let the import of his statements press in upon Chase's mind.

All Chase could think of saying in response was, "How in the world did you get this cell number?"

The president gave a suppressed laugh as he scanned the room of underlings. "Oh, Doctor, if you are a doctor, that was easy," he said without answering his question.

"But now listen. We have someone of great value to you, and if you would let us know the location of the man who is impersonating me, then we can resolve this whole mess quickly and quietly, and you will be given the honors you so rightly deserve. And I might add, have your wife returned to you. You see, we have been monitoring your movements and know what you are attempting to do, but it will never work. It is now one p.m., and if I am correct, you are down to about thirty-six hours before the deadline is up. Time is running out!" the president said, and then the phone went silent.

Chase's cell phone vibrated again. It was another call, but his battery was running low. Dreading what was next, he took the call.

"Hello?"

Without any preliminaries, the vice president began speaking. "Chase, I've got a plan on how we can meet. Listen carefully and take this down." He waited to give Chase time to get a pencil and paper. "Okay, are you ready? I need you to rent a speedboat from the Washington Harbor and make your way up Rock Creek. It is a fairly large estuary that feeds into the Potomac. You can get all the way to Montrose Park by way of Rock Creek."

Chase repeated the instructions as he gave them to make sure he had them correct.

"The Charles C. Glover Bridge crosses over the creek at one point. I'll meet you under the bridge. We can make the exchange there. Then you head back down Rock Creek until you get to the Potomac River and take it to the Tidal Basin. Land the boat at one of the docks and make your way up to the street level. There will be a taxi waiting for you. Take it from Fourteenth Street to Pennsylvania Ave. Turn right and go to the corner of Pennsylvania Ave. and Ninth Street."

Sheriff Conyers and Jennifer leaned in closer and listened attentively as the vice president spoke.

Chase knew the area well having interviewed many lawyers and their clients in front of the J. Edger Hoover FBI Building over the last four years.

"There will be someone inside who will be watching for you. Go with him and do what he says.

Chase cast a searching stare at the two people who he could trust with his life. The tension was palpable, but his thoughts were broken as Randall continued.

"I think it best that you come here under the cover of darkness. It will be a lot harder to see where you are going, but you will avoid anyone who might be watching this place. There is a small dock along that stretch of river, and there will be a red light on the boat dock as you approach from the south. Can you do that?" the vice president asked, his voice carried a sense of urgency and sobriety. The three considered his words for a minute; the sheriff stuffed his hands in his pockets and began pacing the floor, while Chase drummed his fingers on the table. Jennifer was the first to think it through and nodded. The others joined her.

"Yes, sir, but I've got to tell you. This is very risky," Chase said as he read the worried faces of his compatriots. "I just ended the phone with the president asking me, rather, he was demanding me to turn myself in and tell him your whereabouts in exchange for my wife."

It was as if the vice president was standing in the room. His voice had an edge of steel in, and Chase could feel a set of cold, blue eyes bearing down upon him. "Look, Chase, we've got to put them on defense rather than on offense. Right now they are controlling events, but if we can get this damaging information into the right hands, we can turn this thing around. I'll give you a blood sample and the evidence. Then you hightail it over to the FBI lab and let them do the DNA analysis. In the meantime I'll get those who are still loyal to the Constitution lined up to assemble on the steps of the Supreme Courts and demand an investigation into allegations of fraud and treason by this administration. I know that bunch. They will be thrown into a defensive mode. They'll start circling the wagons and closing ranks.

They will immediately begin a smear campaign against me and those Senators and Cabinet Heads who choose to stand against them. They will be so busy doing that, that we should be able to get to the *New York Times* and substantiate our evidence."

There was a beep from his phone, indicating that the battery was about to give out. "That sure sounds like a plan, but without God's divine help, we will fail. There are so many evil men in high places it just like an impossible task." Chase's jaw was set and his eyes bore a steadfast look.

"Well, son, believe it or not, I am a believer in the Lord Jesus Christ, and I know you are too. And I choose to claim the promises God has given in His Word; promises such as, 'Greater is He that is in you than he who is in the world.' I can't count how many times that verse alone has helped me keep my focus on who is really in control of the affairs of this world." The vice president offered, "There is another verse that means a lot to be also. It is in Ephesians chapter six verse twelve. 'For we wrestle not against flesh and blood, but against principalities, against powers, against the rulers of the darkness of this world, against spiritual wickedness in high places.' So Chase," he continued, "the battle is not ours but God's

Chase cast a searching glance at Conyers, his eye as wide as a full moon. "You mean to say that you think this is as much a spiritual battle as it is a physical one?"

It was like history was repeating itself. Chase recalled the tense moments before he entered the conference room in Pastor T.J.'s mansion. The spiritual darkness that pervaded the room, the blindness that each member of the Order experienced, and the coldness that he felt as he raced toward the podium with the Document in one hand and a lighter in the other. He wondered what it would happen next.

His thoughts were interrupted as he heard the vice president shifting in his seat as he considered his words carefully. "Yes, this very much is spiritual warfare. I believe Satan has hated this nation from its founding because it was built upon Christian values and principles. Plus he hates us because ever since 1948 when Israel became a nation, we have stood by her side and have been her friend. Satan hates Israel, and any friend of Israel is an enemy of Satan." Chase sat and listened. His face bore a look of surprise.

"Do you think that the ultimate goal of Satan is the defeat of Israel?" his eyebrows knit together in a question.

"That, my brother, has always been Satan's goal, but the way I read my Bible, it isn't going to happen. When you have the time, read Revelation chapter twelve."

After Chase hung up, he put his phone on a universal charger and turned his attention to begin working out the details of the plan—plans for making a late-night run by boat to the Naval Observatory where the vice president was hiding. They got a map of the area and spent the afternoon scoping out the possible points of departure and course they would have to take, all the while watching the clock wind down. But the stress was getting to Chase, his nerves were frayed, his migraine was returning with a vengeance, and he was losing control,

"We have a problem, guys," said Jennifer as she returned from looking at the television in the police station lobby. "It looks like a large weather system is moving in and it could really mess up our plans."

Chase slammed his hand on the table. "Man, everything's going wrong."

His outburst shocked the other two; his typical good-natured personality was showing signs of wear.

The sheriff looked up from the map, his forehead winkled. "Look, Chase, you need to get a handle on things. You're losing your objectivity."

Chase's face reddened and the veins on his neck stood out like vines. "Yeah, well, I'm also losing my wife. If we don't get these guys what they want, she's dead." His voice came in short, jerky phrases.

"I understand, buddy. But we need to keep our heads, or not only is she going to die but also the vice president and us. They win…we lose, it's as simple as that."

Chase took a seat and rubbed his forehead. "I guess you're right. I was out of line."

Jennifer, knowing how vulnerable they both were to emotional entanglements, was reluctant to get too close. Her heart yearned to go to his side and wrap her arms around him and hold him, but those days were gone. Her chances to build a relationship passed when she left Beaumont years ago. Though at times, she found her mind wandering into the world of *what if.*

The sheriff broke the uncomfortable moment. "Look, if it's all the same to you, I'd just as soon not take a speedboat ride up the Potomac River at midnight in a storm. After having spent fifty years with my feet on solid ground, I'd rather I stay back at the docks and watch for your return."

"That's a good idea, Sheriff," said Chase as he stood and steadied himself on the table. "We need someone to be on the lookout for us when we get back anyway. It might as well be you."

Chase checked his watch. "Look, we better get a move on if we are going to beat that storm."

"Before you go, Chase, you might need this." He handed Chase the gun he used to kill the sniper. It was fully loaded, and the sheriff handed him several more loaded magazines.

Then the sheriff turned to Jennifer and offered her one of his. "No thanks, Sheriff," Jennifer said. "I already have one. As a matter of fact, I have two and plenty of ammo." With that she reached inside her satchel and drew out an Uzi and smiled.

"I am fully trained in hand-to-hand combat and how to use any kind of hand gun. I just hope I don't need to."

Chapter 22

The Naval Observatory...

That night, the heavy weather moved in, and a sweeping rain beat on the windows of the Naval Observatory. The violence of the storm made protecting the property a challenge for the veteran security detail. No one heard the black hawk slip down from the sky and deliver its payload of eight highly skilled operatives.

As the lightning struck a nearby power pole, one of the members of the Delta Force cut the co-axle feeding to the surveillance cameras. The Observatory went blind.

"Sir, we have a video feed failure," said the sergeant to the watch commander. "I think it just got hit by lightning."

The watch commander crossed his arms and looked at his military-issued watch. The hands were illuminated, and he counted the seconds. "In about fifteen more seconds, the backup system should kick in."

It didn't. The power to the whole residence area went down. "Sir, I can't reach the spotter on the roof. I think that we are under atta—"

Just then the blast of a flashbang grenade exploded, stunning the security team in the control center. Then a canister of tear gas was tossed into the room and filled it with its blinding gas. The room exploded in gunfire as men wearing gasmasks and night vision goggles appeared. The NVGs were mounted with a sight red-on-green reticule so that the killers could see their targets and sight in on the red laser beam. The accuracy of these men was 100 percent.

Within minutes most of the security detail were neutralized, and the commandos began moving about the residence—hunting.

Having secured an Express Cruiser Speedboat from the Washington Harbor marina earlier in the day, Chase and Jennifer set out on their journey.

"Just look at those white caps," observed Jennifer as she came down the floating dock.

Chase, who was already feeling a bit queasy standing on the undulating dock, tried to untie the aft rope, looked up. "Yeah, and I can't believe we are doing this at what seems to be the height of the storm.

Just then a gust of wind blew and nearly knocked him and Jennifer off the dock.

The smell of the river mixed with the fresh scent of rain made a palpable impression on Chase. He loved the water but plunging into a storm in a churning river was not his idea of safe, clean fun.

Jennifer, having had more experience, proved to be an invaluable skipper as she guided the boat out into the middle of the channel and opened up the duel 350-hp Evenrude engines.

With the spray from the boat splashing up and the rain pelting them, it wasn't long before both of them were soaked to the skin and shivering.

"I should have worn something heavier than this thin blouse," Jennifer hollered over the sound of the engines and waves.

Chase swiped his hand across his face. His hair was dripping and matted. "Yeah, me too," he said as he squinted ahead. "I hope we can see to find the right creek."

Jennifer, having memorized the contour of the river, shook her head to get the water off her face and eyes. "I think I can find it. It's just up ahead a ways."

They quickly found the mouth to Rock Creek and began picking their way around the twisting channel. After an hour of fighting the swells, making switchbacks, and avoiding large rocks in the water and fallen limbs, they saw a red light on the western bank just before the bridge. As they approached the dock, Chase squinted in the rain and saw a man waving a flag at them. He was one of the remaining members of the security detail, and he had been shot.

Chase got Jennifer's attention. "Head over there to that dock," he hollered over the din.

As they neared the dock, the wounded man reached out his hand and guided the bow of the boat into the boat slip. "Quick, land the boat and come with me. It may already be too late, but we must try," he said as he helped tie the boat down.

"Why? What's going on?" Jennifer asked, gulping for oxygen.

The man's shirt was soaked with rain and blood, and his hair was askew. "We've been attacked by a Delta Force team of operatives. They have cut our video feed and power and have taken out most of the security detail. The last thing I saw was the men fanning out, searching for anything that moved." The man paused a moment to make a cold, professional assessment.

"Go on," Chase prompted.

The agent's face grew dark as he looked at Chase. "Once they have eliminated the resistance, they will blow the door to the vice president and shoot him and his wife. We have got to hurry," explained the secret service agent.

Within a few minutes of landing the boat, they loaded on the motorcycle and sidecar and began making their way across the rain soaked lawns of Montrose and Dumbarton Park. Then they cut across Observation Circle and headed straight for the vice president's residence.

By the time Chase and the others arrived, the operatives had made a clean sweep of the lower levels. After killing the watch command, they made their way to the kitchen. The cooking staff proved to be more resilient than they expected, but out gunned and out manned, they were eventually eliminated. As they ascended the stairs to the level where the vice president's living quarters were located, they met strong resistance. There was a heavy firefight, and the corridors were filled with tear gas and gun smoke. The toxic mix was nearly unbreathable.

The wounds suffered by the secret service agent were not life threatening, and so he led the two back into the mayhem. They entered the lower level, they found the cooking staff all dead. As they made their way through the corridors, it was not hard to imagine what had happened. The Delta operatives were totally unexpected, and almost everyone was taken by surprise. Some people were shot where they stood, and still others who were asleep died in their beds. It appeared that the cooks who were just starting to prepare breakfast offered some resistance but were quickly overwhelmed.

Cautiously, the agent, Chase, and Jennifer made it up to the second and third level. By then most of the gunfire had ceased as the assassins went room to room in search of any more resistance. The agent leading Jennifer and Chase used a mirror to peer around corners.

The first hall was clear, so they cautiously approached the next one. Suddenly, an operative stepped out of a doorway. Jennifer, with her gun at the ready, quickly turned and fired, killing him instantly.

Chase gave her a shocked look.

"I hope that didn't give away our position," she whispered as she resumed her position.

The agent peered around the next corner. Two delta operatives lay dead on the floor, and further ahead lay a member of the vice president's detail. Around the next corner was the vice president's living quarters, and the place where the rest of the protective detail took their stand. All of them were dead, along with three Delta operatives. The remaining two were preparing to blow the vice president's door using C4.

"Within a minute they will blow the door and be in," the agent said to Chase and Jennifer just above a whisper. "We have got to stop them."

One operative stood guard as the other applied the C4As they retreated before the explosion, Jennifer and the agent stepped from around the corner, took aim, and picked off the targets. They fell where they were shot.

The agent's face hardened and he courageously rushed the door but there was not enough time to stop what happened next. The door to the vice president's living quarters exploded, sending shrapnel into the air. What the bullet didn't do to the agent, a piece of shrapnel did. He lay in a pool of his own blood; there was no saving him. Jennifer was blown across the room and hit the opposite wall then slumped to the floor. Her eyes, dazed with shock, pleaded for Chase, someone, anyone, to come and help her. It grieved him deeply to see her lying on the floor, so broken, so helpless, her beautiful features creased with pain. He wished he had his earpiece, stethoscope, and medical kit, but he had none; he was on his own.

He ran to her side, and looked into her dazed eyes. "Jennifer, can you hear me? Where are you hurt?" His heart beat wildly.

Blinded by pain, she blinked and saw Chase in a distance. In agony, she roused and moaned. "I'm hurt pretty badly. Forget about me. Go check on the vice president."

Chase was frantic. "No, I can't leave you here like this," he said as he ripped a piece of his shirt and shoved it in one of the more obvious entry wounds. She was fading fast.

Thinking the danger was over, Chase made a rash decision. "Look, Jennifer, I need to get a medical kit from the infirmary. I'll be back in a minute. You hold on, understand?"

She nodded and tried to smile. Time was running out. He dashed down the hall, turned the corner, and made it halfway down the stairway when he heard voices; it was more operatives working their way back up. *They must have heard the gunfire and are coming as reinforcements*, Chase told himself. He turned and ran back up the stairs, his feet felt like lead, his lungs craved oxygen and his heart felt like it would leap from his chest.

By the time he reached Jennifer, she had already died. Chase didn't have the time to grieve over her; he closed her eyes and turned. The operatives were already coming around the corner. Chase pointed his weapon and fired. The first man fell backward, knocking the second man off balance. Chase jumped through the gaping hole, which once was a solid, oak door. The C4 left little of it. He hit the floor and rolled behind a couch. He knew that within a minute a hand grenade would be thrown in, and his life would end suddenly and violently. He heard a sound to his left. He took his eyes off the door just long enough to see the vice president waving an arm, beckoning him to make his way into a cloak closet. Without hesitation, Chase jumped up and dove into the waiting arms of the vice president.

"Come with me quickly," he said as he closed the closet door. A minute later there was a large explosion just outside the door but the reinforced door held.

Chase gave the man holding him a questioning look. The vice president opened a secret panel, and the two of them slipped behind it, and he replaced it.

"Follow me," he softly said. With that he began descending a flight of steps.

"Where are we going?" Chase asked, his face covered in sweat and dirt.

"This will take us to an escape tunnel. It leads right out to the southern corner of the compound," he said in a low tone.

Within a minute, they reached the bottom of the stairs where the vice president's wife waited anxiously for her husband to return.

After a brief introduction, Chase's eyebrows raised. "How did you know that someone was coming to help you?" Chase asked as they made their way down the dark corridor.

"I'd have to say the Lord prompted me, and I was being obedient to His voice." He said over his shoulder. "When I got to the top of the steps, I heard you talking to your partner. What was her name? Jennifer?"

Chase looked down at his hands; they were covered in blood, her blood. The thought of leaving her lying on the cold floor, grieved him but he had to. He had to finish his mission no matter the cost. "Yes, sir, her name is Jennifer, and she was a very brave woman. She will be missed." Chase choked back his emotions and tried to refocus.

As they approached the exit of the tunnel, the vice president slowed his pace and put his finger to his lips. "Please, be as quiet as possible, they could be waiting for us."

In the dim light, they saw a flight of steps, which led up to the surface. The door was the only thing that stood between them and mortal danger.

"Allow me, Mr. Vice President," said Chase as he eased past him. He quietly opened the door and looked out. It appeared to be clear. He still had his gun and indicated that he should go through the door first and make sure that the coast was clear.

As they stepped from the safety of the tunnel, they were greeted by an unrelenting storm. It had not abated, but rather intensified and sent pea-sized hail down upon the fleeing figures.

Into the storm they charged, driven by fear and survival instincts. They made their way across the two parks back to where they left the speedboat. It bobbed violently in the storm surge as they untied it from its moorings. Then Chase turned the key, and the duel Evenrudes roared to life. He backed it out of its boat slip and carefully eased the watercraft down the river. Chase retraced their course back to the swelling tide of the Potomac River; its black waters threatened to swamp their boat. As they emerged into the main channel, Chase saw another boat sitting out a few hundred yards from shore. He knew instinctively who they were, and what they were waiting for. He jammed the throttle forward and raced out into the channel. The other boat immediately came about in hot pursuit.

The only hope Chase had was to outrun them, but he didn't know how fast the other boat was. He opened up the throttle all the way, and the Cruiser cut its way through the angry waves. Chase turned and saw that his pursuers were gaining. A look of concern filled his face as both boats sped through the inky waters of the Potomac. Shots rang out and bullets whizzed overhead. The vice president and his wife hunkered as low as possible to avoid being hit.

The wind and the rain along with the violent waves made it nearly impossible for the gunmen in the pursuing boat to get a decent shot. But to make it even harder, Chase swerved from left to right. The movement nearly made everyone on board seasick.

Suddenly, a large ship appeared out of the darkness, nearly colliding with Chase's fleeing boat. He cut the wheel sharply to the left barely missing the bow of the tanker. His pursuers weren't so lucky. Chase looked over his shoulder and watched in horror as his attackers were struck amidships causing the fuel tanks to rupture. He blinked and a moment later, an explosion lit up the night sky, and the two halves quickly sunk beneath the dark waters of the Potomac.

Chase slowed his boat down and cruised through the no-wake zone and into the Tidal Basin. He found the boat slip that he and Sheriff Conyers had determined as their point of re-entry and landed the craft. As he turned, he noticed the vice president's wife leaning over her fallen husband.

"Please, he is bleeding badly. I think he's been hit." The lines in her face grew deeper as her trembling hands held her dying husband.

Chase had no time to reflect. He knelt next to Mrs. Randall and saw blood coming from the wounded man's abdomen.

This was the second time in the same hour that Chase wished he had his medical kit; he needed it now more than ever.

"We must get him to a hospital, or we're going to lose him," Chase said to the stricken man's wife.

With adrenaline coursing through his veins, he grabbed the vice president, threw him over his shoulder, and made his way up the floating dock. Sheriff Conyers was watching and came down the dock to lend a hand.

Together, they hauled the wounded man up the ramp and to the police cruiser. By then, they were breathing heavily. "We need to get this man to the first hospital we can find, or we will lose the only living evidence we have," Chase said through gasps.

"Well, we can't let that happen, now can we?" said Conyers as he met Chase's wild gaze.

Carefully they placed the vice president in the backseat and wrapped him in a blanket, which the sheriff got out of his trunk.

Sheriff Conyers looked around and noticed that Jennifer was not in the boat or at Chase's side.

"Where is Jennifer? What happened to her?" the sheriff asked with deep concern in his voice.

Chase dropped his head and shook it slowly. "She didn't make it. She was wounded from a blast of C4 and died before I could administer first aid. She's gone Sheriff...I can't believe it...she's dead." Chase's voice thickened and tears coursed down his cheeks and soaked into his already wet shirt.

Mrs. Randall put a tender hand on his shoulder as he wept bitterly. She didn't speak, but from that one act of kindness, Chase drew strength.

Finally he took a halted breath and looked up then wiped his eyes with his sleeve. "We better be going before we lose the vice president," he said with renewed energy.

Using his GPS for direction and his cruisers lights and siren, the sheriff raced through the rain slick streets of the nation's capital until he arrived at Providence Hospital. He rolled up to a stop in front of the emergency doors. A trauma team rushed from the emergency room, and met them with a stretcher and quickly removed the stricken man from the backseat of the cruiser.

Conyers got out of his cruiser and rushed to the other side as the trauma team was gathering around the wounded man. "This man is under police custody and is to receive a full security team, *stat.*" His voice resonated off the surrounding walls.

The emergency team responded as they were told. Within minutes, as many policemen as there were in the hospital converged in the emergency waiting area.

Conyers did some quick arithmetic. "This isn't enough protection. We need more personnel," said Sheriff Conyers as he dialed a number.

The phone rang, and the precinct chief answered curtly. Conyers ignored his unfriendly greeting. "Chief, this is Conyers again. Would you call up the entire precinct? Have them assemble in and around the Providence Hospital.

"I take it that you found the man you were looking?"

"Yes sir, but he got banged up a bit in the process and he is going into surgery as we speak."

"Oh, I see. Good. Well, give me a few minutes and we'll be there in force."

It wasn't long before the whole department gathered around the hospital. Following the sheriff's instructions, the men and women in uniform formed a perimeter around the hospital. Some gathered on the rooftop, and others took up positions in hallways and even in the lower area where someone might slip in. The hospital was completely sealed off.

As an orderly wheeled Randall into the recovery room, his surgeon stepped to Mrs. Randall's side. "Ma'am, I believe your husband will make a full recovery thanks to the quick thinking of the men who brought him in. His wound, though not life-threatening, caused a lot of bleeding. We will need to keep him here for an hour or so before moving him to a regular room. Is there anything I can get you?" the doctor asked as he took the woman's hand and gently held it.

"No, doctor, thank you for all you've done. He's in the Lord's hands and I'll be alright." Though shaken from the experience, her voice remained steady, confident. She took a seat next to her husband, held his hand, and silently prayed.

It wasn't until he was out of danger that the doctors and staff recognized who he was, or at least who they thought he was.

"Doctor," Chase said, "this man is the real president of the United States." He saw the confusion on his face. "I mean the real…" he paused to rephrase his statement. "Look, Doc, the man who is currently running this country is a fake, a fraud, and an imposter. This man, whose life you just saved, is the real James F. Randall. Now, I know what you are thinking, but the only way to prove that fact is to do a DNA analysis and compare it with the current president's DNA."

The surgeon crossed his arms and looked over his glasses. "Now how do you propose getting a sample of the 'president's' DNA so that we could do the analysis?" the doctor asked flatly.

Chase paced back and forth in front of the doctor, thinking of a simple answer to give to the doctor's question. After a moment of deliberation, he decided to come clean and take him into his confidence. "I am an undercover agent with the FBI. I was inserted into the president's medical team for the purpose of extracting a blood sample."

Then Chase paused and waited for the doctor's reaction. He saw skepticism written on the doctor's face. "How can you prove all this?" the doctor said with a sweep of his hand.

With that, Chase started pulling off his disguise. The first thing he removed was the head piece, revealing a white man. Then came the body building material followed by his elevator shoes. When Chase was finished, there stood a medium-height, white man who was recognizable to all—the noted journalist.

"Sir, my name is Chase Newton."

The doctor was convinced.

It was three a.m. on Tuesday, and Chase had only nine hours to save his wife.

Chapter 23

The Oval Office

"What do you mean you failed?" the president shouted into the phone.

"You assured me that that team of operatives had an impeccable record of success and would eliminate the vice president within minutes of taking the compound." He listened for a moment before letting out a string of expletives.

"Where is the vice president now?" he paused. "You don't know? It's your job to know. Now find him, you idiot!" Then he slammed down the phone. The president stood and began pacing around the Oval Office with his arms clasped behind his back in deep thought.

To one side of the hub of power stood Nguyen Xhu, the president's temporary chief of staff. She hadn't actually signed up for the role she now played but took it when it was offered to her. As deputy to the chief of staff, she served Mr. Edwards. Despite his abusiveness, she served him with a meek and humble spirit. Nguyen was the exact opposite of the now-deceased chief of staff in every way from the perpetual smile, to the kindness in her light, oriental voice, to the faith she had in the Lord.

However, she had one secret, and like an ace card, she held it close to her chest until the right moment. In the meantime, she stood before an angry president as his acting chief of staff and tried her best to serve him.

Nguyen was smart—very smart. As a graduate of the University of California at Berkeley, she held an MA in Political Science and another in History. Her mother and father escaped from Vietnam. Nguyen understood oppression, and she feared what she saw coming if this man was not stopped. She prayed for the right opportunity and for courage to act when the time came.

Washington, DC

The storm that affected the Naval Observatory affected other parts of the sprawling city of Washington, DC. There were power outages all over the city along with numerous fires started by the many lightning strikes. Megan's cell was even darker than it usually was. She could hear fire and rescue vehicles racing to the many trouble spots around her.

With the exception of one, all of her captors were asleep. They had been drinking and playing poker for most of the night and were sleeping soundly. The old, rusty chair had its problems, too. One leg was shorter than the other, and it wiggled and squeaked every time she moved. She figured out that if she twisted her hand just right with a little effort, she could squeeze her small hand out of the handcuff. She moved cautiously. Once one hand was out, she waited. The guard in the other room hadn't heard her movements over the sound of the storm. She tried the other hand and in a moment, it too, was free. After using the rest room several times, Megan had memorized the layout of the building she was being held in. Hers was the last room on the right. There was a front entrance and a back door. Neither was armed with an alarm, but the guard in the other room sat between both escapes. She had been praying for the Lord to deliver her, and she couldn't count the times she thought about the Lord delivering Peter from prison. She knew the passage so well she nearly had it memorized. There Peter sat, chained to the wall with two armed guards standing on either side of him. Suddenly an angel appeared in his cell and bumped him on the side and said, "Get up, put your shoes on, and let's get out of here." Peter couldn't tell if this was a dream or not, but he stood up and started walking. The chains fell off, and the jail cell door swung open. The angel led the way through the first and second ward, and then they came to the iron gate that led into the city. Without a squeak, the great iron gate swung open, and Peter marched right through as free as a bird. That's how she remembered it, anyway.

So she prayed that the Lord would deliver her as He did Peter. As she sat there with her hands free, she suddenly realized that her only guard had fallen asleep, as well. So she gingerly stood up. She took a step. No one heard. She took a second—still nothing. She now was standing at the door of her cell, looking at her sleeping guard. As quietly as a mouse, Megan slipped past the guard and made it to the back door. Miraculously, it opened without a sound, and she slipped into the rainy night and was gone.

Megan wandered down the rain-slick street. She had no idea where she was or what city she was in. With the rain running down into her eyes and the occasional flash of lightning temporarily blinding her, it was impossible for her to recognize the city where she spent much of her time. As panic gripped her heart, she quickened her pace until she found herself running wildly through the lonely streets of the dark city. Occasionally a dog would run after her, frightening her even more. Once she thought she was being followed, she turned to look behind her and stumbled over an empty trash can. The collision sent the can tumbling into the vacant street in one direction and Megan in another. A chorus of dogs began to howl, and she felt she had awakened the whole neighborhood. Her lungs burned, and her feet began to feel like lead, yet she pressed on through the night. She rounded a corner and stopped to catch her breath. Out of desperation, Megan began praying, "Lord, I don't know where I am, and I need you to lead me to safety."

After turning a few more corners and running down several streets, she began to realize where she was. It suddenly dawned on her that she was in Washington, DC. As a child and teen she came here many times and saw all of the sights the city held; the Smithsonian Institute, the Washington Memorial and Reflecting Pool, the Vietnam Memorial along with the Capitol building. She made her way to the one sight that was her favorite. It was the Lincoln Memorial. There he sat, that giant of a man, ever since he took that grand posture on May 30, 1922. She drew strength from the sight of Mr. Lincoln and thought of God. She could see Him through the eye of faith, sitting on His throne, high and lifted up, and the angels circling about crying, "Holy, holy, holy, Lord God Almighty."

She thought, *What a privilege just to know such an almighty,* prayer-answering God. There she stood, soaked from rain and sweat, worshiping her Savior and God.

Chapter 24

The Oval Office...

"She's what!" the president screamed into the phone. Then his eyes grew cold. "Are you even looking for her?" the angry president demanded. *Already it is going on six a.m. in the morning and no word on the whereabouts of the vice president, and now this,* the president thought.

He could see he was losing control. Word on the street had it that there is a press meeting scheduled at ten a.m. to be held on the steps of the Supreme Court. It was to be led by the Secretary of State Bill Ferguson with the Secretary of Defense James Higgins and Secretary of Homeland Security Donald Appleton at his side. The news reported that several key senators and representatives and the Justice of District Court of Appeals in Washington, DC, were going to join them in what appeared to be a "Tea Party"-type rally. The president was clearly worried. He stood motionless staring out the window, which overlooked the White House lawn. Without turning his head, he called sharply to Nguyen Xhu.

He spoke in shorts bursts. "I want you to call an emergency meeting with the Cabinet and joint chiefs.

Also, I want my chief legal counsel in this room immediately."

Nguyen bowed slightly. "Yes, sir. Is there anything else?" She waited as the president continued his gaze.

"No, Miss Xhu, that will be all," he said with a dismissive tone of voice. Nguyen bowed slightly and backed out of his presence. She went to her office and dutifully made the calls.

President Randall's eyes narrowed as he watched Miss Xhu step out of the Oval Office. When the door closed softly, he retook his seat behind the hallowed desk and reached for the telephone. He pushed a button, and a man stepped into his office from another door. The shadow of the man crossed over the president's deck as he took his seat. It was T.J. Richards and he emerged from his hiding place long enough to bring the president a message at the turning of the tide.

An icy look crossed the face of the man sitting across from the president. "It looks like we have a big problem. All that we have been working for is in jeopardy if we don't accelerate our plan. We came so close four years ago. We had the Document in hand and at the last minute lost it only to have it burned before our very eyes. Victory was so close we could taste it. Now after years of planning and preparing, we are close to achieving a major step toward our ultimate goal of world domination, and now this. It is time for phase two, don't you agree?" T.J. said through clinched teeth.

The president nodded. He didn't like being ordered around. He didn't like being a puppet on a string, yet he complied. It was as much out of fear for his own life as it was greed for power.

"Good, then just as soon as the event takes place, you will have the support of the public to implement phase three in an accelerated pace," said the voice with a hiss.

Again the president nodded his acquiescence. He could feel the icy gaze of the dark man's eyes cutting through him, searching him, probing him.

The man rose to his feet and towered over the president. "All right, then, you will be hearing from us shortly." Then he stepped silently out of the Oval Office.

A shrewd smile split President Randall's face. Then his smile transformed into a sneer and then into a cruel laugh.

Chapter 25

The White House...

By seven a.m., the conference room was filled. The closed-door session of the joint chiefs and the loyal Cabinet heads had convened. There was an air of expectancy and the room scintillated with tension. The president was clearly agitated but waited and let the anticipation build before entering the room. There was a threat to his presidency, and he had to act fast. He was looking to these men and women for ideas, for support. He stood and addressed his team.

Everyone stood as he strode into the room and faced the assembled group. His jaw was set, and a look of determination filled his face.

"Thank you. You may be seated," he said in a tone, which belied his boiling emotions. "Ladies and gentlemen, I appreciate you coming on such short notice. In the last hour, I have been given intelligence that may call us to consider raising the threat level." Heads nodded in agreement as many reviewed the prepared sheet with bullet points highlighting the latest developments.

Nguyen Xhu stepped into the room quietly and approached the podium where the president stood. He leaned over to her, knowing already what she was about to tell him. She whispered in the president's ear. "Sir, we have been attacked again!" Then she handed him a sheet of paper with the details.

The president straightened as he glanced down at the paper in his hand. With as much emotion as he could generate, he spoke. "Ladies and gentlemen, I have just been informed that for the second time today we have been viciously and brutally attacked. If what I have just been handed is accurate, the home of the incoming vice president fell under attack earlier this morning by a group of blood-thirsty militants. They killed everyone on the compound. Obviously they were after the vice president, but thankfully he had not moved in yet. And now the latest attack was on the *New York Times* building. Just moments ago, I am told, someone exploded a large car bomb on the parking deck level and has brought it down to a pile of rubble. He paused and looked in the direction of the *New York Times* building. "I have seen that building many times and if this is true, I can only imagine the devastation. I am calling for the threat level to be raised to 'Code Red,' severe risk of terrorist attacks, and a state of emergency to be declared on a national scale. I want curfews imposed and travel restrictions extended. I want this city locked down immediately," the president said with a sense of urgency that the press corps had not seen before.

The initial shock of hearing that one of the most influential news reporting agencies was attacked had a stunning effect. To the men and women in the room, this was personal and it struck them like a punch in the gut. Many wept openly, others stood and blasphemed. Above it all lorded the president; confident, in control.

With his jaw jutted out, he stood and looked down at the cacophony that he was partially responsible for creating and smiled to himself.

The president's chief legal counsel spoke up, "Sir, there are a few legal concerns that I have by imposing curfews and travel restrictions without the approval of the Congress."

The president's gaze swung in his direction and grew cold as ice. "Then let's call for both the House and the Senate to be convened immediately. Those who refuse to respond or those who oppose a unanimous decision to endorse these extreme measures obviously are infiltrators in our government. I want to know who opposes these measures and have them sanctioned, impeached, and arrested for treason. I have known for some time that there are those in my administration who want to see it fail. It will not fail! We will not fail!" he said emphatically. "Anyone who opposes us will be crushed under the wheels of change."

The president paused as if he lost his train of thought—he didn't. Almost imperceptibly the tenor of his voice changed, the look in his eyes grew distant and the focus of his attention—was on the distant horizon. He was a man looking into the very hearts and imaginations of his audience.

"Long have we waited the day when we could emerge from the shadows into the light of the national stage. Too long have our defeats plagued us, haunted us, and have dogged our heels, but no longer. Soon we will forget our sordid past with its defeats. Imagine how different this world would be had history not recorded such defeats as the Battle of Carthage, or our defeats during the Crusader wars, the Battle of Vienna where the Ottoman Turks failed to defeat the Christians, and Battle of Waterloo where our cause was again defeated, our dream destroyed. And who could forget the French Revolution, the American Revolution, and the Battle of Yorktown? If only the tide had turned at Gettysburg, George Washington would have been defeated. If only the course of history would have recorded a different outcome at Antietam, not to mention the First World War and its sister, the Second World War. Imagine how different things would have been if only the Battle of the Bulge had not been fought, or if Stalingrad not fallen.

"All of these were the work of *our* hands. All of these were our attempts to bring about the perfect society, and all ended in humiliation for our cause. But not this time, my friends, not this time. We will rise like a great phoenix from the ashes of history and stretch our wings over the nations of the earth, *and they will fall at our feet*. Now is the time; now is the moment!"

The passion and eloquence of this man crystallized into one mesmerizing chant. It was spellbinding, compelling, and demon possessed. Who was this man? Where did he get such power of persuasion? No one asked, and no one cared as long as their cause was accomplished. There had been other great leaders, leaders such as Caesar the Great, Herod the Great, Nero, Genghis Kohn, Napoleon, Hannibal, Saladin, Togo, Hitler, but none will be remembered for bringing in the new age. There he stood, the president of the United States of America, President James F. Randall, the man who would bring in the Age of Aquarius. The dawn of a new day was approaching, and they were the makers of it. After the president's captivating speech, everyone rose to a standing ovation.

Chapter 26

The New York Times, Washington Bureau...

Utter mayhem was the only way to describe the destruction of The *New York Times* building. Chase, the sheriff, and the hospital staff stood in shock and silence as they observed the ruins on such a massive scale. The *New York Times* building lay in ashes. Police and Fire and Rescue were pouring into the area to try to save the victims and rescue the dying. Ambulances filled the streets. Doctors and nurses from the surrounding medical facilities were rushing to the scene.

Medical teams from Providence Hospital began assembling to respond to the incoming trauma victims. The chief of security had already decided that, despite the risk posed to the vice president; he couldn't turn away the many injured that he expected. To insure the vice president's safety, he moved him into the psychiatric ward, and posted armed guards at every point of entry. Within minutes, the ambulances began to arrive.

Tears streamed down Chase's face as he stood watching the column of smoke rise heavenward and defuse into the skyline. To him, this was the memorial honoring the final sacrifice of his friends and colleagues. By now it was nearly eight in the morning, and the building was filled with secretaries, reporters, editors, and proofreaders. The printing presses would have been running, and delivery trucks would have been sitting at the ready to receive the latest edition. But rather than report the news, the *New York Times* became the news.

Chase's heart was breaking. Everyone that he held dear was either dead, dying, or soon to be dead. First it was Glenn Tibbits, the man that stood courageously against the evils of his day, and then it was his dear friend Stan Berkowitz. Stan drove him to be the best he could be and then some. How he missed him already! Then there was Jennifer, a woman of character and courage. She was truly a virtuous woman, a woman of God. As far as he knew, within the next hour, Megan would be dead, and he was powerless to stop it. How could he get the results of the two DNA tests into the hands of the largest newspaper in the world when its hub lay in ashes?

Chase continued to weep and in his pain cried out to God. He was at the end of his rope. The last night of decent sleep was on the plane, and by now he had been awake for nearly twenty-four hours. He was mentally and physically exhausted, and his faith wavered.

"God, I know that you said, 'All things work together for good to them that love you, to them who are called according to your purposes,' but right now I don't see any good coming out of this. All my friends have been killed, and my wife as far as I know may already be dead, too. It looks like the devil is about to score a big one this time, and I am helpless to stop him." As Chase sat there in one of the recliners in the waiting room, God gave him a rhema, a word from the Word. It was found in 1 Kings 19:18, and it said, "Yet I have left me seven thousand in

Israel, all the knees which have not bowed unto Baal, and every mouth which hath not kissed him."

Chase took courage knowing that there were still many who had not surrendered their senses to the whims of societal evolution. A peace came over Chase's troubled heart, and he fell asleep.

Chapter 27

The Joint Houses of Congress…

It was going on nine a.m., and Chase woke to the sound of the president of the United States of America as he addressed both Houses of Congress and the American people.

There he stood, flanked by the people who plotted and planned the demise of the nation they were sworn to protect. He approached the podium and looked into the soul of America.

"My fellow Americans, today our homeland has been struck again by tragedy. Forces within our borders who oppose this administration and who have worked long and hard to see it fail have lashed out against us. These are the same people who claim to love and pray for our country, who wave the American flag the most vigorously, and who fill the airwaves with the constant rants against the perceived shortcomings of this government, this administration. They oppose free speech, oppose the rights of a woman to choose, and stand against the rights of our elderly to choose when and how they will die. They are not the real Americans. They are not the true patriots. They seek to divide us over trivial things such as religion, creation versus evolution, abortion rights versus the rights of the mother, conservative versus liberal, and the list goes on and on. They claim that if you don't agree with them, you are un-American. Well I'm an American, and I don't agree with them. As a matter of fact, the vast majority of Americans don't agree with them, and so what does that make us? Traitors? No, my friends, I submit to you that they who would wish us failure are the ones who are the traitors of America.

"So today I am submitting to the congress new legislation that will weed out those who would seek our defeat and bring them to justice. In essence, this new legislation will require everyone to obtain a 'Citizenship of the World' card. This card, which will have a PIC, a Personal Information Chip, can be obtained by swearing allegiance to the United States of the World. With this card, you will be given all the rights offered to you as an American citizen. You will be allowed to buy and sell and participate in commerce as you always have. You will be allowed to conduct your affairs just as you always have, only on a grander scale because you will be a citizen of a much larger family, the family of the world. If you refuse to swear allegiance to the United States of the World, you will soon run out of money, your bank accounts and all assets will be frozen, your driver's licenses will no longer be valid, your credit cards will not be accepted. You will be hunted down, imprisoned, tried for treason, and shot. Also, as a part of this sweeping new legislation, we are breaking off all diplomatic ties with the State of Israel. I have instructed the Ambassador to Israel to return to the United States without delay. I have been given evidence, irrefutable proof that it was members of the Masad,

Israel's elite delta force, who perpetrated this unprovoked attack upon this nation."

"Far too long has the Israeli government provoked their peace loving neighbors with their inflammatory rhetoric. Far too long have they flaunted their very existence in the faces of our friends, the Palestinians, the Syrians, and our friends the Iraqis, and have built settlements in the occupied lands which do not belong to them. This must stop!"

He interrupted his diatribe for a moment to allow his teleprompter to advance before continuing.

"Effective immediately we are calling for the withdrawal of all Israeli military and civilian personnel from the Golan Heights, from the West Bank, and from the occupied areas. Also, we are demanding reparations be made to those affected by their senseless and willful disobedience to World Law. If Israel refuses to comply within the next forty-eight hours, I am authorizing our military leadership to begin to draw up plans that would include the neighboring countries of the State of Israel to join us in enforcing World Law.

"I also have signed into law a national curfew and declared a state of emergency. This will effectively stop all interstate commerce and travel. This state of emergency will only be lifted when the population comes into compliance with the new standing law of the land."

Again he paused and let the spontaneous applause subside.

"Now I know that these measures that I have taken may seem harsh, and for the short-term they may even be painful, but in the long run they will pay great dividends. When all of these malcontents are removed from our midst, we will then have the perfect society that we all have longed for. This perfect society will allow you to become whatever and whoever you long to be. To express yourself in any way you think best without the old Victorian values that have been imposed upon us, we will finally throw off the restraints, the chains, and the shackles that have held us back. We will truly be a free society."

As he concluded his comments, the whole congress stood to its feet in thunderous applause. The president stood basking in his glory. *I have opposed the God of heaven and have gotten away with it,* he thought as he stepped off of the platform. *What power. With the stroke of the pen it's the law of the land. Indeed the pen is mightier than the sword, especially when I am holding the pen!*

He had won!…or so he thought.

Chapter 28

The Oval Office...

As the president returned to the Oval Office after giving his speech, Nguyen handed him his usual cup of hot tea. It was a tradition with this president to sooth his dry throat with hot tea after every speech.

"Thank you, Miss Xhu. That will be all," he said with the wave of his hand.

She bowed politely and started to back away. "One more thing, Mr. President," she said, looking at the floor.

His eyes narrowed and he turned impatiently. "What is it, Miss Xhu?"

She hesitated, knowing the kind of response she would get. "It's the Internet. News about a conspiracy theory is spreading across it like a wild fire, and there are people converging on Washington from all over the country. As we speak there is a gathering of senators, members of the House of Representatives, and even some from your Cabinet on the steps of the Supreme Court. They are standing in opposition to the measures you have just proposed. There is a press conference scheduled for two o'clock this afternoon."

The president let out a string of expletives that cursed her Lord and Savior. Righteous indignation swelled within her spirit, but rather than lash out, she demurely retreated into the background and prayed for his soul.

The president had a problem, and he needed to fix it quickly before it spread. He sipped his tea and picked up the phone. "Get me the National Guard," he demanded and slammed down the phone.

Within a minute the commander of the Washington, DC, brigade of the National Guard was on the phone and received his orders. President Randall leaned into the phone and spoke through clenched teeth. "Get down here and restore order. Anyone who resists you, arrest them. If they get out of hand, use whatever force you deem necessary to quash this rebellion."

"Yes, sir," was all he heard before the phone call ended abruptly.

This threatened all he had worked for, all he dreamed for. His anger was palpable as he stepped into the anteroom off from the Oval Office.

Within an hour, tanks and armored personnel carriers began to converge on the chanting, singing, praying masses. Undeterred by the threatening show of force, the courageous people of America stood their ground.

The tea Nguyen prepared for the president was an old recipe made from leaves and herbs found native in Vietnam. But the president had an allergic reaction to it, causing him to have a fatal heart arrhythmia. Before he could call for help, he collapsed on the floor of the anteroom.

Moments after his body fell to the floor, he heard a voice. It wasn't the voice of Miss Xhu, neither was it his personal secretary. It was the voice of Him who holds the universe in His hand. "You have been weighed in the balances and have been found wanting…this day your soul is required of you." In a moment President Randall stood before the Sovereign God of the universe.

No one found the president's body for several hours, and by then Nguyen Xhu had left the premises.

Immediately upon hearing the president's address to the nation, it was broadcast to the world. Nations began moving men and material into position in an effort to force the Israeli government to comply with World Law. The madman of Iraq readied his nuclear missile launchers. The moment he prayed to Allah for had finally come. He would personally lead his forces across the Syrian Desert and into the land of Israel. The Russian government began transporting vast amounts of land forces through the Republic of Georgia, having virtually stripped the tiny nation of any military resistance on August 8, 2008. The Palestinian blockade was penetrated and fresh arms began to pour into the Gaza Strip. Israel who was already surrounded with hostile nations now found herself drifting alone in an angry Arab sea without a friend in the world.

Chapter 29

The Lincoln Memorial

Megan woke to the sound of sirens. The morning broke bright and clear and except for the smoke-filled air it would have been a delightful day for a walk in the park. As her mind cleared, she thought, Where am I? And what am I doing here in the Lincoln Memorial? Then she remembered. She had escaped from her abductors and wandered through the night and ended up here. She'd spent the night within the safety of this gentle giant. Now she wondered, What's going on? Why the sirens, and where is the smoke and debris coming from? Fearful yet inquisitive, Megan stood and began to make her way in the direction of the smoke. The closer she got, the more she recognized the area. It was downtown Washington, DC, and this was the area where her husband worked. She saw the twisted street sign bearing the name G Street. Were it not for the smoke, she could have seen the White House. The closer she got to the center of the activity, the more fire and emergency vehicles she encountered, the thicker the smoke became, and the more she recognized the area. Then it suddenly dawned on her that the source of the smoke and debris was her husband's office building, *The New York Times*.

Fear gripped Megan's heart and she swallowed hard to suppress the lump in her throat. She shuttered at the thought of her husband and his colleagues being incinerated in that firestorm. Tears streamed down her face as she thought about losing her husband without having one last opportunity to say, "I love you." Suddenly Megan felt vulnerable and exposed. And though there were hundreds of people all around her, Megan stood in the midst of the chaos and for the first time in her life felt all alone.

With the announcement of a state of emergency being declared and a curfew being imposed, the American people were thrown into a state of confusion. Employees didn't know if they should leave their place of work and get home or stay and finish out the day. Shop owners didn't know if they should close for the day or try to maintain the work schedule. In many cities, unruly mobs flooded the grocery stores and bought or stole all that was on the shelves. Within the day, grocery stores closed their doors and boarded up their windows. In many cases there was no hope of reopening them because no shipments would be permitted to enter the state to re-supply them.

Street gangs began roaming the city streets, plundering and looting as they went. No one was safe to walk the streets as they fell into their clutches.

Neither was Megan safe. It would only be a matter of time before a marauding gang would catch her, or the police would arrest her for violating curfew, or her abductors would find her and recapture her. Yet there she stood on the corner across from where her husband once worked, staring, hoping, and praying that she would awake and find this to be an awful nightmare—it wasn't.

Throughout the day, television crews and radio announcers scoured the area, covering the mayhem. As one particular cameraman panned the area for background footage, he serendipitously caught Megan's face in his lens. Immediately her image was relayed to the television station and flashed across the nation. There she was in plain sight for all to see, all including the Dean, her former abductors…and Chase. What started as a simple act by the cameraman developed into a life-and-death race to obtain this one person who held the key to the future. The question was, who was going to get to her first?

Immediately, the Dean and a team of cutthroats began racing to the scene of the explosion. Chase woke up the sheriff who was catching a few moments of sleep. The two of them raced to the street corner where Megan was last seen. Hope swelled in Chase's trembling heart; if only he could get to her before her captors did. Hate fomented in the heart of the Dean as he thought of the last time his cause was thwarted by Megan and Chase.

Through the smoke and haze, the figure of a man emerged behind Megan.

"Ma'am, would you mind coming with me?" said a rather well-dressed gentleman. The bulge under his tailored suit told Megan that he was carrying a weapon and that it probably would not be a good time to for her to run.

Her took a sharp breath and covered her mouth. "Why? Where are you taking me?" she demanded. The man ignored the question for the moment as he nodded in the direction of the car.

Megan was in panic mode; her mind raced as she thought what she should do. She consider running but quickly ruled the idea out. There was something about the look in the man's eyes that told her that it was no use in resisting, so she meekly complied. Who is this man? And what does he want with me? He isn't one of the thugs who had been holding me captive, and he clearly isn't an official policeman, she thought to herself. Without speaking another word, the man in the suit led her to a waiting car, opened the front passenger door, and nodded for her to get in. Megan hesitated then demurely got in. The door closed with an assuring thud, and her escort stepped around to the driver's side.

He got in and put the car in gear.

"Ma'am, I am one of the few men left of the vice president's security detail," he said quietly. "He has asked me to escort you to a safe house where we can offer you protection and care for your immediate needs. Would you permit us to do that?"

Megan turned to the man with a look of genuine awe. The vice president? She blinked absently then nodded and slumped back into the cushioned seat, not knowing whether to laugh or cry.

The secret service agent put the car in gear and gradually pulled away from the curb. His movements were smooth and professional, and it occurred to Megan that he was not a threat to her. A cloud of smoke drifted across the street and the car was gone.

Chapter 30

The Street Corner…

Megan watched the scene of the tragedy pass behind her just as a black Volvo turned the corner. Megan recognized the driver as being one of the men who had held her captive.

The Volvo came to an abrupt stop, and two men jumped out and raced to the intersection; they found the corner vacant. The Dean ordered his driver to get back into the car and circle the block a second time while he looked for Megan. With so many emergency vehicles parked precariously, it took ten minutes for his driver to come back around the block. By that time an old police cruiser pulled up and its occupants got out and began to search the area. The billowing smoke drifted across the intersection, and the cruiser disappeared from sight.

On the adjacent corner stood a well-dressed young man who was looking around as if he were lost. It was obvious by his demeanor that he was unaware of any danger.

The advantage was clearly on the side of the Dean as he approached the young man from the back. If he acted quickly, he could capture Chase and force him to lead him and his men to the vice president. Cautiously, the Dean circled around to the left and allowed a wisp of smoke to come between him and his prey. Although he didn't usually carry a weapon, since he had gotten into the abduction business, he began carrying one wherever he went. As he approached the young man, he drew his gun, pointed it at him, and spoke.

"Well, Mr. Newton, we finally meet." His voice curled into a sneer. "Put your hands up and turn around slowly."

The man slowly raised his arms to the air and turned, revealing a frightened elderly man in his fifties with rimless glasses that enlarged his gray eyes. The Dean's jaw dropped and his eyes went wide. This isn't Chase, he thought, this was just an innocent bystander, and I'm standing here pointing a gun at him. The Dean read fear in the stranger's eyes and savored the moment. Both men were in a difficult position. *Should I continue to play out the game? Should I shoot the man where he stands?* The Dean chose to latter.

Again a cloud of smoke swept across the street corner and enshrouded the two men. It was as if the world had closed its eyes to any more death and destruction.

The silhouette of a man appeared in the haze, and a shot rang out. The Dean stood, holding his weapon. His eyes bulged, the color of his face paled and he staggered backward as he tried to regain his equilibrium. His chest was covered in blood. He turned and raised his gun with his right hand and fired wildly. Another shot rang out and struck him with deadly force. His body fell to the ground with a sickening thud and was surrounded by a growing pool of his own blood.

Rarely had Sheriff Conyers seen such disbelief on another man's face than on the Dean's. His eyes were fixed upon the stranger holding a gun. He didn't know him, but it didn't matter anymore. The Dean, the man behind much of the chaos in the world, lay dead in the street. Sheriff Conyers lowered his sidearm and returned it to its holster. Then as he stepped up to the dead man and kicked the gun from his hand, leaned down, and checked his pulse. There wasn't one. Within seconds a TV crew and a number of police officers assembled at the scene.

Chase stood on the opposite corner and watched the drama play out between the sheriff and the Dean. Later he testified to a grand jury investigating the shooting that the sheriff shot a well-dressed man as he attempted to rob an innocent bystander. Because of his uniform and badge, there were few questions, and soon Sheriff Conyers returned to his vehicle only to find it empty.

A search of the area uncovered no clue as to the whereabouts of his friend. He frantically dialed Chase's cell phone; he got no answer. All attempts at locating Chase proved to be fruitless.

It seemed Chase simply had vanished into thin air.

Chapter 31

Providence Hospital...

As the events unfolded on the street corner, other events were taking place a half block away. The vice president's body guard drove up to the police cruiser. He rolled down his window, and Chase peered in. He recognized him and quickly got in without asking any questions. To his surprise and relief, he was greeted by the slender arms of Megan as she greeted him with a shower of kisses. Then the car disappeared in the smoke.

The smile in her lovely eyes turned to a flicker of hope as she hugged Chase. "Oh, Chase, I've been so worried about you, and that evil man, the dean, wouldn't let me talk to you."

Megan buried her head in husband's chest and inhaled the warmth of his body. Her heart beat wildly as she held him close.

Chase felt her trembling body against his. Her skin was still cold and damp from the elements and he rubbed his hand on her arms to warm them. It was a reunion he would never forget as he kissed away her tears.

As the driver maneuvered through the menagerie of abandoned cars, his phone vibrated. He tapped his Bluetooth earpiece.

"Yes, sir, I got her and a bonus…"

Chase and Megan could only hear one side of the conversation. "No, sir, not the Dean, but it is someone I'm sure you will be glad to meet…" He paused for new instructions. "The Providence Hospital?" the driver thought a moment. "Yes, sir, I'll come as quickly as I can," he said as he tapped his earpiece again, ending the conversation. Then he changed lanes and took the highway that led to the hospital.

Megan turned to Chase with a confused look on her face. He reached over and brushed the hair from her eyes and put a finger to her lips.

"Sir, ma'am," said the driver as he peered into the rearview mirror, "I just got a call from the vice president asking me to return to Providence Hospital. I hope you don't mind."

Megan placed her hand on Chase's arm and clutched his shirtsleeve. "Chase, what is going on? I don't understand," said Megan, her eyes wide with confusion.

"M," Chase said in a calm voice, "you wouldn't believe it, but during the last ten days our nation was under attack, and you were in the very eye of the storm."

She sat up straight and gasped. "I was? Who were those men that abducted me, and why did they want you?"

Chase looked deeply into her eyes and contemplated how much to tell her. He knew the pain it would cause her to tell her about the loss of her friends Glenn and

Jennifer. He also knew that eventually he would have to tell her but not then. Too much hung in the balance.

Her next question brought him to his senses.

"What does the vice president have to do with all this?" The tension in her voice begged an answer.

The battery of questions was overwhelming, and Chase didn't know where to begin, and so he simply kissed her and took her in his arms.

"I assure you, M, I'll explain everything as soon as we get to the hospital, okay?" Twenty minutes later they exited the freeway. As they approached the hospital, the security detail opened the parking gate and let the car pass through.

Megan clung to her husband's arm as they entered the hospital lobby and took the elevator up to the floor where the vice president awaited them. He pushed himself shakily to his feet as they approached. Vice President Randall reached out and took both of their hands in his and greeted them.

"Mr. and Mrs. Newton, it is so good to see you," the vice president said sincerely. Chase gripped his hand firmly and looked him in the eyes. Then the vice president wrapped his arm around Megan and gave her a fatherly hug. "I am so sorry that you were dragged into this mess. I can't imagine what you must have gone through, young lady. I must hear all about it in time." Then he smiled and looked at Chase and said, "I owe you my life, Chase, and the country owes you a huge debt of gratitude."

"Thank you, Mr. Vice President, but it isn't about me. A lot of good people paid the ultimate price to get us this far." His throat closed with emotion.

Megan stood with eyes as wide as an owl. She had never seen Chase as emotional as this before and it jarred her. "Oh Chase, I can't imagine."

Mrs. Randall, who had been standing next to her husband came and put an arm around Megan's slender waist. "Don't let him fool you; your husband is a very brave man."

The vice president's face darkened. "Well, it may be too soon to start popping open the champagne." He paused and looked at the television in the corner. "We still have an angry sitting president to deal with." He paused and looked away; his piercing eyes had an interesting glint in them.

"Keep going Mr. Randall," Chase said. His voice etched with concern. "Level with us."

"The doctors say I'll make a full recovery from the wounds I received in the speedboat chase. They also inform me that my wounds are in the exact location as that of the president's. If it weren't for the protective body armor, the bullet would have killed me, but by God's grace it didn't. That got me thinking…"

For the next thirty minutes, he mapped out a new strategy for saving the nation. But time was of the essence.

Chapter 32

Hours Earlier

With the announcement of the new order being imposed upon society, there were new restrictions. These were not just travel restrictions but restrictions of the press and free speech. Television stations and radio stations fell under new and very restrictive rules. Talk show hosts were the first to feel the muzzle. Within the hour of the news conference, many radio stations were locked down, and many of the popular talk show hosts were arrested before the stations could mount a counterattack. Fortunately, the Internet had not felt the pinch yet, and the counter attack began there.

Hours earlier, Chase had opened up Glenn's laptop and logged on to the Internet. He found a string connecting to the now infamous "WikiLeaks" and downloaded all the files onto that site and the information went global. Bloggers began picking up the information and, after doing a bit of authenticating its veracity, spread the information even further. By nine a.m., everyone who had access to a computer knew of the conspiracy in our government, and by ten a.m., cars, buses, and RV campers filled with loyal, red-blooded Americans began descending upon the nation's capital. They came from all over the country, even as far away as Texas and Nevada. They came and filled the mall and lapsed over into the streets. Soon the capital and White House areas were inundated with angry Americans, and they would not—they could not—be stopped.

In Congress, the opponents of the president's mandates were easily defeated, and the new bill was quickly enacted. The proponents of the Constitution were immediately labeled as dissidents and troublemakers. But before all of the new regulations kicked in, they took one last stand by calling for a two o'clock press conference on the steps of the Supreme Court. Surrounded by a gathering chorus of peaceful demonstrators and antagonistic press, the courageous senators, representatives, and Cabinet heads stood shoulder to shoulder in the spotlight. Each one in turn stood in front of the microphone and read from notes from Glenn Tibbit's computer file. Others read from the Constitution and pointed out the places where the president and the out-of-control Congress had overstepped their boundaries. Together they demanded the impeachment of the president and for the members of his cabinet to step down. With this new information, they called for their colleagues in the Congress to reassess their support of the state of emergency and called for the lifting of the curfew and sanctions against Israel.

As Secretary of State Bill Ferguson spoke before a mesmerized audience, a black limousine with United States flags on its front fenders slowly pushed its way through the throng. It was flanked by an army of

Secret Service agents, and the crowd reluctantly parted, letting the oversized Cadillac through. The presidential limousine continued to make its way through the mass of people until it stopped directly in front of the podium. Secret Service agents stepped to the side of the automobile and opened the door. The image of the president of the United States of America emerged from the shadow of the vehicle. He stood erect and straightened his tie as he scanned the unfriendly crowd. He frowned back at their angry faces. Immediately the crowd began to boo his appearance. The president seemed impervious to the rejection but rather stepped up to the speaker and quietly asked if he might have a word with the American people. Demurely, the Secretary of State yielded the floor to the president.

The president surveyed the masses before speaking. Then in a clear voice of authority, he began to address the people.

"Ladies and gentlemen, citizens of this great land," said the president, "within the last hour, I have been informed that those whom I have trusted to keep me informed with the most accurate and honest information have been deceiving me." He paused and let the suspense build.

"But since I am the president, I take full responsibility for my actions. I acted upon misleading and fallacious information, and so, effective immediately, I am rescinding my call for a state of emergency, and I am lifting the curfew. Within the hour, I will be calling my dear friend, the president of Israel, and make a full apology for maligning his character and motives. I am prepared to send whatever support our friends in the

Israeli Defense Force, might need to stand against the aggressors surrounding them. I am calling for Russia and the Iraqis to cease and desist all military actions against our friend, Israel. To proceed against this peace-loving nation will be the same as attacking our land. As one of our flags of history once said, 'Don't Tread on Me.'" The president paused and let the applause subside and then continued.

"The Personnel Information Chip, as I have been informed, is intrusion into the privacy of the American people, and I am calling for an immediate recall of this device. I am also appointing a Blue Ribbon Committee to investigate those in my administration who have been working behind my back to bring about the demise of this great land. And so, my fellow Americans, breathe the fresh air of freedom."

To his delight, the audience who had booed moments earlier now cheered him. How easily swayed these people are. They are like sheep having no shepherd, he mused.

"And let me assure you, my fellow Americans," his voice boomed, "I will be relentless in my pursuit of the truth and ferret out every traitor to the Constitution, so help me God." His eyes bore a look of determination. Again the audience cheered and spontaneously broke out singing "God Bless America." The president paused while the audience cheered and then continued.

"I am also taking measures for the immediate removal of the current vice president and will be appointing my good friend and colleague Bill Ferguson, the secretary of state, as my acting vice president until the Congress approves him. As all of you know, there have been rumors of a great conspiracy, something about DNA and me not being who they say I am. Well, let me assure you, I am President James F. Randall, the real James F. Randall, and to prove it, I am calling for Dr. Cleve Newberry, the man who is responsible for saving my life, to step to the podium."

Out of the crowd of people stepped a well-built black man dressed in a medical overcoat. He stepped smartly to the platform and was followed by a nurse.

The president greeted them warmly. "Sir, could you state your name and occupation for the press?"

He stepped closer to the microphone and addressed the audience, "Good afternoon, I am Dr. Cleve Newberry, and I am the doctor who treated the president in Mogadishu when he initially received his injury. I was there to assist him on Air Force One and see that he was stable before returning to the scene of the ambush and rescuing the remaining security detail, including my nurse assistant, Miss Hodges. I stand here today and can confirm that this man is indeed James F. Randall, the president of the United States. I also am holding in my hand a copy of the DNA results proving that he is who he claims to be," and with that said, Dr. Newberry raised the evidence up for all to see.

The jubilant throng went wild. Cheers and a long ovation followed as the men on the steps watched the mood of the country change from fear to hope and from hope to celebration. A new day dawned across the land.

As the president retook his position behind the microphone, he continued to address the people of America. Chase and Megan, flanked by Sheriff Conyers and the Secret Service agent, stood, cheered, and hugged and waved American flags. But it didn't go unnoticed by Chase that as the president spoke, he lightly touched the top of the podium with the tips of his fingers.